A PASSIONATE CAUSE

Recent Titles by Aileen Armitage from Severn House

ANNABELLA
CAMBERMERE
JASON'S DOMINION
MALLORY KEEP
A PASSIONATE CAUSE
THE RADLEY CURSE
A THEFT OF HONOUR
THE SEAMSTRESS
A WINTER SERPENT

A PASSIONATE CAUSE

Aileen Armitage

This title first published in Great Britain 2000 by
SEVERN HOUSE PUBLISHERS LTD of
9–15 High Street, Sutton, Surrey SM1 1DF.
Originally published 1971 under the title
King's Pawn and pseudonym *Aileen Quigley*.
First published in the USA 2001 by
SEVERN HOUSE PUBLISHERS INC of
595 Madison Avenue, New York, N.Y. 10022

British Library Cataloguing in Publication Data

Armitage, Aileen
A passionate cause
1. Historical fiction
I. Title
823.9'14 [F]

ISBN 0-7278-5630-8

For my jewels...

Printed and bound in Great Britain by
MPG Books Ltd, Bodmin, Cornwall.

ONE

THE spring sunlight glinted on the blade of the hatchet upraised in the peasant woman's brown, muscular arm. Topaz watched the arc of its descent and heard the thud as the blade neatly severed the chicken's head from its body.

'Fine dinner that'll make ye, Fräulein Birke,' the woman grunted, and Topaz nodded. She was reaching into the pocket of her skirt for the coins to pay her, when she heard the woman's quick, indrawn breath. The chicken's quivering body had leapt upright. Silently it ran four, five, six shaky, unbalanced steps and its claws touched damp straw.

As if trained by a lifetime's reactions, the headless body no sooner felt the straw beneath its feet than it squatted, strained, then fell over and remained inert on the straw. An egg rolled slowly down on to the cobblestones and cracked.

'Mother of God,' muttered the old woman, hastily crossing herself. 'An omen if ever I saw one. Pray heaven 'tis not an evil sign.'

Topaz felt a surge of anticipation replacing the dullness she had felt up to the moment of the chicken's surprising feat. Wondering, she watched the old woman wrap the chicken and place it in her basket, and having paid her, she pushed her way through the throng in the market place.

On the road home Topaz gathered her cloak more tightly about her, for the April wind was still cool, whipping up little clouds of dust along the hedgerows. 'St. Teresa,' she cried aloud, for there was no one on the lonely road apart from herself, 'you heard my prayer! One little sign I begged of you, to show that this year at last something exciting would happen, and no sooner have I left the church and gone into the market than this chicken'—she glanced at the contents of her basket—'performs in death what only the living should do. Oh thank you, St. Teresa, now I can wait in peace.'

It was late afternoon by the time Topaz had covered the five dusty miles home, for Torwald was an isolated house set deep in the lush countryside. Her stepfather, she knew, would be waiting impatiently for her return. As she turned into the gateway she saw his scowling face at the parlour window.

'So you're back,' he grunted as she entered the gloomy oak-panelled room. Topaz surveyed him silently. In all her seventeen years she had never known Kaspar Birke to smile or soften his hard expression in any way.

'I've got a fine chicken for our supper,' she said quietly, folding her cloak. Kaspar looked up sharply.

'You've been to the market! I've told you there's no need for you to go there!' he growled, placing his muscular arms akimbo. 'There's servants to go to the market. You were going only to the church to be shriven, in preparation for your Easter duties, you told me!'

He eyed her suspiciously. Topaz sighed.

'I did so, stepfather, then I thought I would bring you a surprise.'

'I do not want you to be seen in the market place, I've told you! There's too many idle fellows hanging about, and foreigners too. I don't trust all those foreigners. Many of those English people living here while their King is exiled come over the border from Holland, and I don't trust those Englishmen.'

'Nonsense, stepfather. They hardly ever come here.'

Seeing his face darken, Topaz picked up the basket. 'I'll take the chicken down to the kitchen and see to the supper,' she said lightly, and swept out.

She was lucky. The words were out before she could stop them, and it was a wonder he had not struck her for her insolence.

She watched Hannah deftly clean and stuff the bird. Hannah was one of the few remaining servants now that Kaspar's fortunes had fallen so low, and she was finding this large house difficult to maintain with only Topaz's help, for Topaz's older sisters Perle and Saphir had married and left.

Unable to keep the secret she was hugging to herself, Topaz told Hannah about the miracle sign of the chicken.

'Holy Mother of God!' breathed Hannah, her pale blue eyes wide in astonishment. 'That can only be a sign of great good or great evil about to befall!'

'I believe it will be a great blessing,' Topaz declared firmly. 'Something wonderful is going to happen—and soon. This year is going to be a wondrous year, I know it. I shall always remember the year of Our Lord 1659.'

Hannah smiled indulgently. 'I hope you are right, child,' she said.

'I am, I know it! Saint Teresa heard my prayer!'

Topaz laughed happily and pirouetted round the deal table, her dark woollen skirts flying out about her. For the first time she could remember, she felt eager expectation for what life held in store for her.

In the morning Topaz gazed out of the mullioned window of her chamber. The leafbuds were burgeoning fast and translucent pale green leaves appearing on the trees. The air had that soft shimmer of awakening spring, and Topaz's spirits had risen with the sap.

The house was buzzing with expectant activity too. To

everyone's surprise the usually surly Kaspar had read his mail that morning and then pleasantly ordered the household to cleanse and sweeten the house against the arrival of a guest. A guest! After all these years! Topaz was content. The magic was beginning. So many years of loneliness since her mother had died, and then Perle and Saphir had married, and not once had Kaspar permitted a visitor to the gloomy house.

Topaz sang as she opened up the fusty, damp guest chamber, removed the dust sheets and opened the windows wide. She shook out the hangings, choking in the clouds of dust that rose from them.

Who could the visitor be? No doubt in the fullness of time Kaspar would overcome his natural secretiveness and tell her who he was, and when he was to be expected.

Hannah bustled in.

'All must be swept and scrubbed, polished and aired,' she said briskly. 'There's no time for daydreaming, Topaz.'

She spoke kindly but with the air of authority of a mother, for such she had become, in effect, since Topaz's own ailing mother had died when Topaz was barely three years old. 'Ask Hans to bring up kindling for the fire,' she said, flinging wide the doors of the huge carved press in the corner, and putting in sachets of lavender.

Having given Hans his orders, Topaz found her stepfather at prayer in the little room they used as an oratory. She saw him kneeling before the statue of Our Lady of the Sorrows, and turned to leave silently, but Kaspar rose stiffly from his knees and turned to her.

'You too must pray,' he said to her solemnly. 'You must do penance for exhibiting yourself in the market place yesterday. I can permit no impure thoughts or actions in this house, now above all times, when I am to bring a lady guest into the house.'

'A lady, stepfather?' Topaz could not help the surprise in her voice. Kaspar made no secret of his abhorrence of women, evil but necessary creatures, vain and selfseeking. His irritation at being saddled with three stepdaughters when his wife so thoughtlessly died, had only been softened by the eventual marriage and departure of two of them.

'Indeed, and why not?' Kaspar said crisply.

'No reason, stepfather. Indeed, I shall be glad to have company,' Topaz answered.

Kaspar turned away without comment. At the door he hesitated, then turned.

'Tomorrow I ride for Munich. In a week I shall return with Frau Secker. See that all is as befits a lady when we come, but do not seek our company. I shall be obliged if you would keep to your chamber so far as it is possible during her stay.

'That is all. Now to your prayers, my girl, and seek forgiveness for your brazenness.' Abruptly, he was gone.

Topaz could not hasten to Hannah fast enough to tell her of the visitor. She found her pounding spices in the stone-flagged kitchen.

'Frau Secker?' Hannah mused. 'Now I wonder what Herr Kaspar has in mind with her?'

'You know her?' Topaz asked eagerly.

'She was kinswoman of your mother's. Her family was wealthy too. I fancy Herr Kaspar minded not which of the two he married, so long as he acquired their money. Much good it did him, though. He had no head for business matters and soon squandered your mother's dowry away. Now it would seem he's after Frau Secker's too.'

'But—she's *Frau* Secker,' Topaz interrupted. 'She is married, is she not?'

'Widowed, less than two years ago, I heard tell.'

Topaz contemplated a moment. If her stepfather was wooing the lady, it would account for his ordering her to keep out of sight.

Hannah paused in her pounding again and looked up thoughtfully.

'Aye, she's a wealthy widow now, and what's more, Frau Secker is still only in her thirties—young enough to bear him a child yet.'

'A child?' Topaz could not follow Hannah's reasoning.

'That's one thing your stepfather never forgave your mother, that she never bore him a son. Not a living one, that is,' Hannah corrected herself. 'God knows, she travailed hard enough, poor soul. In all the Rhineland there wasn't a dearer, kinder woman, so willing to forgive.'

Hannah's eyes moistened at the memory. Often before Topaz had heard Hannah speak of her stepfather's harshness to her mother, but on being pressed for details she had merely pursed her lips and said it was not for young ears. Evidently she thought otherwise now.

'As you know, Topaz, your own father died in a hunting accident, and your mother gave birth to you a few weeks later. Poor Margrete! She was near out of her mind, poor lamb, she loved him so. I well mind the day she visited the fortune teller, on her wedding eve, and he foretold that her happiness was not to last long. Thereafter, he said, Margrete's only treasure would lie in her children, no matter what worldly wealth she possessed.'

Hannah paused and wiped the back of her hand across her eye, leaving a smear of saffron on her cheek.

'She called her babies her jewels, and named you all three after them, Perle and Saphir and you. Until your father died there was great happiness in this house.'

'Then why did she marry Kaspar?' Topaz asked.

'To give her babes another father, she said. Kaspar was pressing, and well he might be, for Margrete was both pretty and rich. Small and slender she was, like you, and with the same deep honey-coloured hair and fine brown eyes. But gentle, oh so gentle. . . .'

Hannah picked up her pestle again and beat her anger out on the spice in the bowl.

'No sooner was he installed in her house than we saw the real Kaspar,' she muttered viciously as she pounded. 'He took over her lands, her money, her servants, and treated her no better than a skivvy. A son he wanted, above all else, to inherit all that which he had just acquired, so it would not go to you girls.'

'And Mother could not give him one?' Topaz ventured.

'Five times in a little over two years he made her with child,' Hannah snapped. 'Each one she lost. No sooner was she staggering from her sick bed, thin and wasted, than he took her to bed again, the brute. Four times she miscarried, and each time Kaspar grew angrier and more cruel.

'She begged for a little time to recover her health, but there's no mercy in that grim soul. The fifth time she carried the babe full term, but grew frailer and weaker in the attempt.'

There was a strangled note in Hannah's voice as she saw again in her mind's eye the poor wretched girl's labour.

'She was brought to bed one fearsome night when a storm was raging. Kaspar was raging too. A son, he demanded, a living son she was to bring forth, or he would curse her for ever. She uttered her last gasping breath in her struggles to bring it forth. We drew from her dead body—a dead son.'

Hannah could speak no more. She turned away and fussed busily over the spit to hide her emotions. Topaz too could scarce resist weeping for the misery of the mother she could not remember.

Hannah came back to the table in a moment, when she had regained control of herself, and rested her large, capable hands on it.

'I think even Kaspar began to realize after that he had gone too far,' she went on. 'In his own way he tried to assuage his guilt by becoming as religious as Margrete had been. He took to dressing soberly in dark colours, fasting often, and spending many hours on his knees in prayer.

'He found good husbands for Perle and Saphir, but in that I think he still had his own advantage in mind, for their husbands were wealthy enough to relinquish their wives' share in Torwald. Now only you remain, Topaz, who has a prior claim to the estate.'

At last Topaz saw the significance of Frau Secker.

'I see. . . . And if he marries again and has a son. . . .'

'And he can find a rich husband for you. . . .'

'Then all is secure for him,' Topaz concluded. Then the next logical step occurred to her. 'Has he a husband already in mind for me, Hannah?'

'That I know not, but I am sure he keeps you hidden from public view so that you will not interfere with his plans, my child. It would not suit him at all if someone were to come seeking your hand who had not the riches he would require. But come, we waste too much time in idle conjecture, child. There is work to be done.'

And Hannah was her usual brisk, busy self again.

Topaz watched the tall, broad figure of her stepfather disappearing over the hill on horseback the following morning, and breathed a sigh of relief. A whole blissful week without his repressive, dominating presence stretched ahead of her. He could bring Frau Secker, marry her if he would, but Topaz was free to breathe, to suck in the fresh spring air and be herself for the next glorious seven days.

As a first gesture of freedom, she reached up and drew out the tortoiseshell combs which bound her hair, holding it tightly drawn up. She luxuriated in the feel of the thick, heavy tresses falling freely in waves over her shoulders, and tossed her head happily in the warm sunlight.

Now to get out of this black stuffy gown with its tight sleeves and rigid stomacher, she thought. Something gayer and looser, so she could run in the fields and feel the sunlight on her bare arms, that's what she'd wear.

She turned from the gate to recross the lawn to the house, but the sound of distant hoofbeats made her stop. Strangers rarely found their way to this remote spot—who could it be?

Presently along the lane two figures on horseback appeared, cantering wearily and kicking up clouds of dust around them. As they approached nearer she saw they were two men, one probably twenty years older than the other, and both looked weary and travel-stained.

They reined in their horses as they drew level with the gate. The older man doffed his hat and spoke in very halting German.

'Your pardon, Fräulein, but could you tell us how far it is to the nearest inn?'

Topaz heard him, but her eyes were on the younger man. He had long glossy black hair, his own, not a wig, and he was rather shabby, but his keen dark eyes showed his evident interest in her.

'Ask her if we might not stay here, James. She's the prettiest wench I've seen in miles,' he murmured in English, and drew his horse round to approach closer to the gate.

Topaz smiled with pleasure. 'Thank you sir,' she replied in precise, clipped English. 'The nearest inn is at the village five miles away.'

Both men stared, then smiled.

'How did you come to speak our tongue?' the older man asked.

'I was well tutored in my youth,' Topaz answered. 'If you

care to dismount and rest here a while, I should be glad to bring you some ale and food to eat.'

They needed no second bidding. The younger man dismounted and stood facing her across the gate. His head was a clear twelve inches above her own, and as she looked up into his clear, sombre eyes, far darker than her own, she felt a shiver of anticipation.

Fleetingly the vision of the chicken crossed her mind and disappeared, but in some way Topaz knew that the events the omen had presaged were connected with the handsome young man standing expectantly before her.

Topaz did not hesitate in her decision, whether to continue the old life or embark on the unknown.

'Please come in, gentlemen,' she said, opening the gate.

TWO

THE strangers comfortably seated in the parlour, Topaz hastened to the kitchen.

'Hannah! Hannah!'

Hannah's flushed face looked up from the beef she was tossing in a skillet over the open hearth.

'Lord have mercy! What's all the fuss about?' she demanded.

'Visitors, Hannah! Two English gentlemen! They're in the parlour, and oh! so weary and hungry! You must draw some of our best ale for them, quickly!'

Topaz rushed to fetch two pewter tankards from the dresser, and in doing so, the aroma of the beef in the skillet, mixed with fragrant herbs, caught her attention.

'And food for them too, Hannah. Is that our midday meal? May I give it to them?'

Hannah, who had been too overwhelmed by Topaz's unwonted excitement to speak hitherto, rose, pan in hand, and faced her squarely.

'Now hold hard a moment, mistress. Am I to understand you have invited strangers—foreigners at that—into the house in your stepfather's absence?'

She looked sternly at Topaz. She might have no love for Kaspar, but unseemly behaviour behind his back she would not permit.

Topaz put down the tankards and came round the table to Hannah.

'Oh Hannah! If you were to see them, you would take pity on them too! Their eyes are red-rimmed with fatigue, and I know they are gentlemen! Their clothes are well cut, though shabby, and they are so polite!'

Topaz's eyes were round and pleading, and she knew Hannah would not be able to resist. 'Come now, where's your compassion, Hannah?' she said persuasively.

Hannah was not to be won over so easily however. She tossed the contents of the pan thoughtfully for a moment, then said, 'Well, since they are in, you had best return and talk to them, as befits the lady of the house. I shall bring up some ale for them, and then I may see them for myself.'

Topaz thanked her and hastened back to the parlour. The younger man was standing at the window, gazing out at the view, while the elder of the two sprawled in a velvet-covered chair. He stood up as Topaz entered.

'Hannah will bring you ale immediately,' Topaz said, indicating to the gentleman to be seated again.

'Madam, you are most kind,' he murmured. 'Pray forgive me, I have not introduced ourselves—this is Charles Barlow, and I am James Butler.'

Both men bowed. Topaz inclined her head.

'And my name is Topaz Birke, stepdaughter of Kaspar Birke, in whose house you find yourselves, gentlemen. I regret Herr Kaspar is away on business at the moment.'

She was aware that Charles Barlow was regarding her quizzically, but so far he had made no attempt to speak to her.

'You are on your way to the Dutch border, I take it, Mr. Barlow? On your way to The Hague, perhaps?'

The two men looked quickly at each other.

'To Rotterdam, Fräulein—on matters of business,' responded Barlow. She noted the deep velvety quality of his voice, in keeping with his sombre eyes.

'Come Charles, you are somewhat curt with the lady,' James Butler quipped. Barlow recovered his composure quickly and moved towards Topaz.

'Madam, forgive me. I was bereft of the power of speech, overcome by your fair beauty. I hope you will pardon my abruptness?'

He bent low over her hand and kissed her fingertips, and Topaz felt a tingle run up her arm. Hannah chose that moment to enter, bearing a tray with the foaming tankards of ale.

Both men drank deeply, while Hannah stood and surveyed them from the corner by the door.

'Ah! The finest, coolest ale I've tasted in many a long day,' said Charles Barlow with a sigh of satisfaction. 'Is it of your own brewing, mistress?' He addressed Hannah.

Hannah's plump face dimpled. 'Indeed sir,' she said, and bobbed him a curtsey.

'Then mistress I salute you! A finer ale-brewer I have yet to discover. James, a toast to Mistress Hannah!'

Both men stood, raised their tankards to Hannah, then drank the remains of the ale. Hannah flushed with pleasure. No one had complimented her so in many years.

'I shall be glad to bring you more sir, along with the beef,' she murmured, covered in confusion, then fled the room.

Topaz smiled inwardly. Charles Barlow's charm had evidently softened the heart of even prejudiced old Hannah, for she had decided to have them stay to eat.

After the meal Topaz excused herself from the men and went down to the kitchen.

'Poor souls,' said Hannah as she placed the greasy platters in the bowl, 'They needed that meal, and they look worn out, both of them. They must have been riding all night. Could do with a good night's sleep, I'll be bound.'

Topaz looked at her expressionless face, trying to read her mind. Was Hannah suggesting they might stay here, but did not want to say it openly?

After a moment Hannah went on, 'After all, what the eye doesn't see. . . .'

That *was* what she was suggesting! Topaz was delighted. So long as the men were gone within a week, Kaspar would never need to know. She hugged Hannah and ran back upstairs.

'Madam, your generosity is overwhelming,' said Charles Barlow in reply to her invitation, 'and in truth there is nothing I should like more than to rest here a day or two and enjoy your ravishing company. But I fear there is business James and I must attend to.'

James Butler cut in. 'I, at least, have to be in Rotterdam ere tomorrow nightfall, Charles. But there is no need for you to haste away.'

Charles looked down at the floor uncomfortably. 'There is the matter of money. I regret, Fräulein Birke, our travels have impoverished us somewhat, and. . . .'

Topaz interrupted him angrily. 'Sir, I did not invite you to stay in return for payment, but as my guest. This is no common inn. However if you do not choose to accept my invitation. . . .'

Charles stood towering above her, remorse in his dark eyes. 'Mistress Topaz, forgive me. The last thing in the world I would wish to do is to offend you. Please attribute my clumsiness to my fatigue, if you can.'

Topaz felt guilty. 'Of course, you must both be utterly jaded. It is I who should beg your forgiveness, gentlemen. Pray allow me to show you to your beds. After a good sleep, Mr. Butler may feel better able to continue his journey, and you, Mr. Barlow, may decide as you wish.'

But remembering the admiring look in his eyes, and the

pressure of his fingertips on hers, Topaz secretly believed Mr. Barlow would choose to stay a little longer.

The next few days brought an unexpected foretaste of summer to the little Rhenish valley, and after James' departure for Rotterdam, Topaz went for many long walks with Charles Barlow in the rich green countryside. He was professedly very fond of exercise.

'God, but it's beautiful here,' he murmured one day as he lay on the turf chewing a blade of grass. 'It brings back memories of the lush English countryside I knew in my youth. Oh the peace and solitude, Topaz! I would I could know such peace and contentment always!'

He rolled over on his back and surveyed her. Topaz was sitting upright, her arms clasped round her knees and her hair blowing freely in the breeze. She too was feeling the same deep contentment. Over the last few days an easy, warm relationship had grown up between her and Charles. Despite his air of sadness he had a graceful charm and Hannah was now completely ensnared by his courteous manner.

'How long is it since you saw your own country, Charles?' Topaz asked him.

'Twelve years.'

'Have you been in Holland ever since?'

'No. I've covered the best part of Europe in my travels, but nowhere have I found the peace that is here.'

After a pause Topaz went on, 'Twelve years is a long time. You must have been only a child when you left home.'

'Hardly a child. I was sixteen, near enough. Not much younger than you are now, Topaz.'

'And your parents? Are they in Europe too?'

Charles sat up and looked across the valley.

'My father is dead,' he said quietly. 'My mother and sister live in France and I rarely see them.'

Topaz looked at him in surprise. 'But are you not anxious

to see your mother?' she asked, then added quickly, 'My own mother died when I was a baby, but I think I would have been glad of a mother's comfort.'

Charles smiled ruefully, but the smile did not reach his eyes. 'I fear my mother has precious little concern for me,' he said, then seeing the shocked look in Topaz's eyes he added, 'But let us talk of other matters. Like your beauty, Topaz.

'How is it you are so slight and lovely? Most of the German women I have seen are large-boned and heavy, solid women who look fertile and peasant-like. But you—just look at you! A puff of wind could carry you away!'

He took her hands and drew her to her feet, then put his hands round her tiny waist and whirled her around. Her skirts flew up in the breeze and her hair tumbled across her face. Topaz laughed aloud with pure pleasure.

Then he set her down again, his eyes once again serious and thoughtful. 'You're a witch, little Topaz, out of some ancient German legend, come to tempt me to stay and forget the outside world, lost in your beauty.'

'Like the Lorelei?' she teased him, gazing up at him.

'No. On second thoughts, you're a ministering angel, come to pour balm on a wounded soul.'

'Are you a wounded soul, Charles?' She raised a hand to brush back his glossy, windswept hair from his face.

'If only you knew.' He took her hand and put it round his neck, then folded her gently in his arms.

Topaz felt alarmed, but as his mouth tenderly sought hers, then her neck and shoulders, she felt a rising excitement, growing into a shuddering thrill. She trembled violently.

'Come, my dove,' he said, his voice low and hoarse, 'I would not hurt my little bird. Oh Topaz! If you knew how I loved you!'

Strangely perturbed by his touch, yet unwilling to make him stop, Topaz finally pushed him away.

'Forgive me, Topaz,' Charles murmured. 'You have been so kind to me, I felt you really cared about me.'

'I do, believe me I do!' Topaz protested.

'The years I have wandered over Europe, unloved and unwanted, save by the harpies one can find anywhere who will sell their embraces for hard cash,' he went on, as though to himself, 'and at last I felt I had found someone whose soul was in accord with my own.'

He looked sadly down at her, his hands at his sides. Topaz felt guilty and cruel. She took his hand and pulled him to sit beside her on a grassy hillock.

'Oh Charles! I'm sorry! I did not mean to hurt you!' she cried anxiously. Charles sat sorrowfully beside her, his eyes large and pleading as a spaniel's. Topaz's maternal instincts were awakened by his pathetic look of mute appeal.

'Do not look so sad, you are not unloved and unwanted here,' she said softly, and seeing the eager light rekindle in his eyes she went on, 'Hannah and I both love you fondly.'

'Hannah? Oh, Hannah is a dear creature, bless her, but your love would mean everything to me. Do you love me, Topaz?'

Topaz had never before felt this strange mixture of compassion and excitement for anyone. It was a strange, intoxicating feeling—what else could it be but love?

'Yes Charles, I think I do,' she said at last, very quietly.

Charles uttered a sound that could have been a cry of triumph or a moan of anguish, and covered her hands with kisses. Then, very gently, he put an arm about her shoulders and pulled her down on the grass, raining kisses on her face.

Topaz was ecstatic. She loved and was loved by the most fascinating man in the world. She luxuriated in the gentleness of his hands, caressing her, as loving as a mother's touch, she thought.

But then his hands became more urgent, more exploring,

and Topaz was shocked when he pulled at her bodice and groped inside. But the sensations he aroused in her were so pleasing that she did not stop his hand.

'I love you, Topaz, I love you,' he murmured between kisses.

'And I you, Charles,' she murmured dreamily.

When Topaz sat up some time later and smoothed down her gown and her rumpled hair, she had the odd sensation of having just woken from a blissful dream. What had just occurred had the half-remembered unreality of a dream, all violence and ecstasy, but so natural.

Charles lay supine, his arms under his head and his eyes half-closed against the sunlight. The tall grass all round them swayed and swished in the breeze, and Topaz wondered why the lush verdant meadows had never seemed so beautiful before. She rolled over on her stomach and regarded Charles soberly.

'I do love you, Charles.'

'I know. And I love you.'

'In a few days you will be gone and Kaspar will return. Will all be as it was before you came here?'

Charles smiled lazily up at her. The dark fire in his eyes was gone, and they were as cool and thoughtful as before.

'Can it be the same for you again, Topaz?'

'No,' she said decidedly. 'It can never be as it was. But will you come back again?'

He laughed. 'Never fear, little one, we shall meet again. If by some stroke of chance we English should inherit our own again and return to our own country, you can always track me down in London.'

He smiled again at the serious look on her face. 'Come, this is no time to talk of separating. We have two more days together before that time comes.'

She relaxed, and leaned over him to tickle his long nose

with a blade of grass. He jerked his head away, but she persisted. He sneezed, then laughed and caught her wrist.

'Mistress minx,' he said, 'I'll teach you to torment me,' and he pulled her down to him again.

That night Topaz sat on the window seat in her chamber and gazed out at the stars. Bless you, St. Teresa, she murmured, you sent me the sign and then kept your promise. The most exciting thing of my whole life has come to pass—I love Charles, and he me.

Topaz had spoken not a word of what had passed to Hannah. In any event, how did one find the words to express what had passed between her and Charles? Topaz had never known such bliss existed. Possibly Hannah could guess by her flushed face and happiness that Topaz was in love. Soon, perhaps, Topaz would tell her.

As she undressed for bed and brushed out her long hair, Topaz thought of Charles, now in his bed, and hoped that this night at least he would sleep untroubled by the fear of being unwanted and unloved. Soon she was deeply asleep.

On the far side of the house, Charles was lying awake in his bed. A clatter of small stones on the window pane made him leap to his feet, and hasten across to the window in his nightshirt. James Butler's face, white in the moonlight, was staring up at him.

'Come away quickly, Charles, there's no time to be lost!' he called up, softly but urgently.

Charles dressed quickly, then hesitated. He scribbled a hasty note at the desk by the window, then glanced around the room before leaving.

Outside, James was waiting for him, with two horses ready saddled.

'Events in England are moving fast, Charles,' James said. 'Cromwell's parliament is running into heavy weather. The army is restive, the more so because its pay is sadly in arrears, and the Commons are on the point of attacking military rule. Between the army and the Commons, Cromwell is lost. Mordaunt thinks the moment is ripe for a royalist uprising.

'It is imperative we move fast. It is near on a hundred miles to Rotterdam, so we must ride hard tonight. Come!'

Hannah came in and drew back the curtains in Topaz's chamber. The sunlight streamed in across the bed-hangings. Topaz rolled over and stretched lazily.

'Here's a note I found in the parlour,' said Hannah. 'I can't read it—it's some foreign gibberish. I'll go waken Herr Barlow now.'

Topaz sat up and read the note.

> 'I regret James came to call me away on urgent business which could not wait. I shall never forget your kindness to a man in so much need of love and comfort. Au revoir, my little Topaz, my jewel.
>
> Charles.'

Topaz's dream world dissolved instantly, like spring snow under the hot sun.

THREE

MORDAUNT'S attempts to co-ordinate royalist risings in various parts of England misfired. News of the plot leaked out and the uprising was cancelled. Thus, some weeks after leaving Torwald, Charles and James were still in Holland, at the court of Mary, Princess of Orange, in Breda.

'That's the last game of tennis I play with you!' gasped James as the two men left the tennis courts and sat on a rustic seat. 'You thrash me soundly every time. God! I would I were as young and fit as you are!'

James fanned his flushed face vigorously with his hand. Charles laughed, his teeth flashing whitely in contrast with the brownness of his skin, but it was a mirthless laugh.

'The Lord knows why I bother so much about keeping fit,' he said. 'To what end, I often wonder. Merely to be able to keep on roaming the world, begging and scrounging? 'Tis an insult to a man's dignity.'

James looked at him quickly. Charles was evidently in one of his depressed moods again.

'Why man, you must needs keep fit, to be able to lay every pretty wench we meet!' he joked, and clapped Charles jovially on the shoulder.

'Come now James, do not exaggerate. Not every wench is to my taste, I assure you. Please allow me some sense of discrimination,' Charles retorted.

'That reminds me, Charles. I meant to ask you—what about that fair little wench just over the border—did you take her? I often wondered.'

Charles frowned. 'Which one?'

'The little puritan thing who gave you shelter in that god-forsaken spot—where I came in the night to fetch you.'

Charles' brows rose as he recollected. 'Ah—the little maid with the name like a jewel! I remember she begged a lock of my hair as a keepsake.'

'Did you give her one?'

'Not I! If I left a lock of hair at every port of call I'd be as bald as a coot in no time!'

'Well, you didn't answer my question, did you lay her?'

Charles smiled knowingly. 'You would not have me betray a maid now, would you?'

'I'll be bound you did, though,' James replied. 'In truth, your stamina amazes me. Europe must be liberally sprinkled with your bastards by now.'

He looked sideways at Charles, to see whether he might look angered at James' impertinence, but Charles only smiled his slow, indolent smile.

'While there are women to open their arms to me, and who excite me, why should I not find what happiness I may? I warrant you, they enjoy the experience too.'

'But have you never truly loved a woman, Charles?'

'I love each one—madly—at the time.'

'But only until she has given herself to you.'

Charles laughed again. 'You are too much the moraliser today, James. I think you would be better suited to Cromwell's puritanical régime in your present mood. Come, let us go in search of a good draught of ale—that last game has given me quite a thirst, I declare.'

Topaz's sadness at finding Charles so suddenly gone was not wholly unrelieved. The sun shone less brightly and the spring had lost its patina of promise, but the parting, she felt sure, was only temporary.

He had said 'au revoir' and not 'good-bye' in his letter, had he not? And in the meadow he had sworn they would meet again. But when?

'Oh St. Teresa!' she prayed fervently in the little oratory. 'Pray let it be soon!'

Kaspar returned, triumphantly escorting Frau Secker. Topaz was not sorry she was banished to her room, for Frau Secker had a cold, unsympathetic manner.

'I reckon Herr Kaspar will have found his match in her,' commented Hannah drily one day. 'He'll not find her so easy to part from her money as your mother was. She's got a good business head on her shoulders, that one.'

Topaz felt guilty at keeping Kaspar in ignorance of the strangers' visit, but he was obviously so engrossed in Frau Secker after his return that he had time and attention for little else. Hannah and Topaz were thus able to keep their secret.

But the weeks slipped by and the weather returned to its normal, springtime changeable nature. Topaz sat in her chamber and watched the grey drizzle outside that seemed to reflect her mood. Life was empty and grey without her beloved Charles.

Hannah was very concerned for Topaz.

'What is it, love? You have no mind to anything these days,' she asked, a frown of puzzlement furrowing her brow.

' 'Tis nothing, Hannah, do not fret,' Topaz sighed.

'Come, shall we refurbish your bed with the new hangings I brought from the market? Or would you like me to get you some fresh lace for your Sunday gown?' Hannah racked her brain for some means to divert Topaz from her gloom, but to little avail.

The weather brightened and became warm again. Topaz was helping Hannah in the kitchen, straining jelly while Hannah was deftly slicing raw beef on the chopping board.

All at once Topaz felt dizzy, then the stone flags of the kitchen floor suddenly seemed to dance. She groped for the edge of the table to steady herself, but blackness swam before her eyes, and without a sound she slid to the floor.

When she came to, Hannah's anxious face was bending over her, and she was loosening Topaz's bodice and fanning her vigorously.

'Topaz, my pet, are you not well? Is the heat too much for you? Come, I'll get a glass of canary for you.' She drew the still faint girl to a high-backed stool near the door.

'Thank you, no, I am well again now, 'Tis as you say, the heat and a too-tight bodice, I'll warrant,' murmured Topaz. 'A breath of fresh air is all I need.'

But despite fresh air, Topaz still felt queasy and faint. She tried to hide her discomfort but Hannah's wary eye noted her grimace of distaste when she looked at the raw beef.

Suddenly, to her dismay, Topaz retched violently and vomited. Hannah ministered to her, then sat by her side thoughtfully.

'It can't have been the neat's tongue; we all ate the same and it has had no effect on Herr Kaspar or Frau Secker. Nor was the milk curdled.'

Her brow was drawn sharply into a frown of utter bewilderment. Topaz felt a pang of compassion for her.

'Do not fret, 'tis not your cooking that is at fault, Hannah. 'Tis more like I have a touch of the ague,' she said gently.

Hannah leapt to her feet. 'Then to bed with you at once, Mistress Topaz. I shall bring you some posset, then you may sleep.'

She fussed anxiously over Topaz, until she was satisfied she was comfortable and feeling better. She tucked the counterpane tightly in, smoothed her pillow and left her to sleep.

The following day Topaz seemed to be her normal self

again, and with misgivings Hannah allowed her to get up. But no sooner did Topaz smell the odour of roast pigeon and sauerkraut than she promptly felt sick again.

Hannah saw her tortured expression. Her face crumpled, then suddenly brightened. 'I have it! The flux! It is the time of the flux with you, is it not?'

Topaz shook her head.

Hannah looked at her curiously. 'How long is it since you had the flux?'

Topaz tried to remember.

'It was when the pedlar came—remember? You bought some laces and ribbons for my gowns from him.'

Hannah was at once deep in thought. 'That was the day I was brewing the ale—let me see——' She calculated slowly, using her fingertips. At last she announced, 'That was seven week ago.'

Topaz nodded. 'I suppose it must be.'

Hannah looked a shade suspicious, and rather uncomfortable. After a pause she asked in a rather offhand way, 'Have you felt any other odd sensations of late?'

Topaz considered a moment. 'No, none I think. Apart from one day when I had the strangest feeling of fullness and tightness here——' she indicated her bosom, '——and such a tingling. But it soon passed.'

Topaz was not prepared for Hannah's reaction. The old woman's hands flew to clutch her head, and she rocked herself to and fro.

'Dear God! Forgive me!' she cried. 'Let it not be! It cannot be!'

'What cannot it be, Hannah?' asked Topaz in alarm. 'Have I got some terrible disease? Oh Hannah! Tell me quickly!'

'First you tell me,' said Hannah, recovering herself. 'There has been in this house but one man—Mr. Barlow. I must know what passed between you and him while he was here.'

Topaz flushed with embarrassment. 'I love him, Hannah. I meant to tell you ere now.'

Hannah laughed mirthlessly. 'Any fool with half an eye could see that, the way you've moped and pined since he left. But what did you do together?'

Topaz smiled dreamily as she remembered. 'We walked and talked, we laughed and sang. Oh Hannah! He is so gay and carefree when the cloud of depression lifts from him.'

'Walked and sang—what else?' said Hannah remorselessly.

'He kissed me.' Topaz's eyes were downcast, a pretty blush on her cheeks replacing their earlier pallor.

Hannah, not to be diverted by Topaz's evident embarrassment, plied her with questions until she had elicited what she feared.

'Mea culpa! Mea culpa!' groaned Hannah, flinging herself on her knees on the cold floor and clasping her hands in supplication. 'Forgive me, Lord, for my omissions! I should have taught the maid the ways of the world ere now!'

'Hannah—what is it?' Topaz cried.

'The brute! The unspeakable brute!' Hannah wailed. 'Taking advantage of a poor ignorant maid for his pleasure! The swine! And he a guest in the house too!'

Topaz was terrified by now. 'Hannah, for pity's sake, tell me! Have I caught some dread disease from Charles?—no, I refuse to believe it!'

'Heaven grant you have not, my child, though even that is possible with a devil such as he!' Hannah spat viciously. 'A devil with such a fair face and charming manners—he cozened us both.'

Topaz, her face covered in tears of fright, said piteously, 'Then what is it you fear, Hannah? Pray tell me!'

Hannah faced her and placed her hands gently on Topaz's shoulders.

'I fear he has got you with child, Topaz.'

Hannah was beside herself with terror lest Kaspar should discover the reason for Topaz's indisposition, but still he was fully occupied with Frau Secker.

'There is still time to put matters right,' Hannah muttered late that evening, and she pulled her cloak over her shoulders.

'Where are you going?' Topaz asked.

'To see Mother Stegner—she has a cure for all ills,' Hannah answered.

Topaz's eyes opened wide. 'But she is a witch, so they say! Are you not afeard to go to her, and at night too?'

Hannah shook her head. 'She knows many country remedies, herbs and the like, that have been handed down to her through the generations. She'll do us no harm if we pay well enough, and 'tis like she could do us some good.'

She hurried out into the night, and Topaz crossed herself and prayed for Hannah's safety. Few dared venture near Mother Stegner's decrepit little old cottage deep in the forest, and those who did had to be in dire straits indeed. It was with great relief, watching through her chamber window, that Topaz saw Hannah creeping stealthily back into the house some time later.

'What did she say?' Topaz asked eagerly when Hannah knocked quietly at her door and slipped in. 'Can she put a spell on me, or give me a potion?'

Topaz was not altogether convinced that she wanted to do whatever Mother Stegner might advise. She loved Charles dearly and would be glad to bear his child, but if bearing a bastard was going to anger Kaspar to the point of frenzy, then what was she to do for the best?

Hannah did not give her time to debate the matter.

'Mother Stegner has told me what to do. You are to bathe in water as hot as you can bear it, then sit on a pan of hot coals. If that should fail, then I have a potion which will do the trick.'

Satisfied that she had the answer, Hannah began heating water for Topaz's bath.

Later, scalded and scarlet, Topaz obligingly sat on the warming pan, which was near red-hot with its contents.

'Aaaah!' she shrieked. 'My skin is blistering!'

'That cannot be helped,' said Hannah, pushing her firmly down again.

But in the end Hannah had to give in. Topaz, blistered and scalded, was obviously going to remain pregnant.

'Then there's nothing for it—we must take the potion,' said Hannah. Topaz was too exhausted to argue. She took one sip—then spat it out.

'Dear heaven! What is it?' she asked. ''Tis poison!'

'Don't waste it, it cost me a gold crown!' Hannah exploded. 'Drink it down at a gulp. I know 'tis a vile brew, but if it works, 'twill be worth it.'

Bravely, Topaz drank it down. But by next morning there was still no sign of the flux.

Time slipped by. Topaz was resigned. Now there was no decision for her to make. She would have to bear Charles' child. The only question was, how long could she and Hannah keep Kaspar in ignorance? Frau Secker's visit was coming to an end, and before long Topaz's condition would be obvious to the world. If only there was some way she could contact Charles and tell him of the child. She felt sure he would marry her at once, but how on earth was she to find him?

Charles tossed a handful of cards on to the baize-topped table.

'I give in! You have me soundly beaten, James.'

James smiled. 'That atones for the beatings you always give me at tennis. That makes—let me see—twenty seven pounds you owe me now.'

Charles pulled a wry grimace. 'You'll have to be satisfied with an IOU. God, I think half my kingdom will be already pledged to pay my debts if ever I regain my throne.'

'You'll have to find yourself a wealthy bride then, Charles,' James smiled.

'Are you seriously suggesting that, as my adviser?' asked Charles.

'Why not?'

'Have you anyone particular in mind, may I ask?'

'Well, there's the Princess Henrietta.'

Charles pulled a face of distaste.

'Come now, she's not so unattractive,' James remonstrated.

'She's passable, I suppose, but her mother, the Dowager Princess—have you ever met anyone so overbearing, James? She's a dragon, that woman, she dominates Henrietta's every move.'

'But if you're really so much in despair about your financial position, it would be an advantageous economic move, Charles, don't you agree?'

'You are right, of course. But the idea of taking that horsy wench to bed does not appeal to me at all.'

James laughed uproariously. 'Come now, you have never confined your lovemaking to one woman before, and I doubt that you will do so after your marriage, no matter how desirable your wife might be. That's no argument against the proposition at all.'

Charles fell silent for a while. Eventually he looked up. 'Well, I suppose royal marriages are always made for political reasons and not for love, and it seems I shall be no exception. As is your wont, you old fox, your head rules your heart. You're utterly right, of course. I shall begin paying my attentions to the lady—and her fiendish mother—at once.

'God knows, I should be glad to have some money in my pocket to call my own again.'

Topaz woke in the night, bathed in cold perspiration and trembling from head to foot. She stared in terror round the chamber, and its familiarity gradually calmed her.

She had been dreaming—of the chicken that laid an egg after its death—but this time the scene appeared to have a sinister feeling about it.

The omen that she had happily accepted as a sign of good seemed suddenly to have changed into a premonition of danger. She felt afraid now, both for herself and for the babe she carried, and prayed long and anxiously to St. Teresa before she could go to sleep again.

FOUR

KASPAR at length escorted Frau Secker back to Munich, then returned to Torwald. After letting household affairs take their course unsupervised so long, he was anxious to have account rendered to him.

He sent first of all for Hannah and after reading her accounts he scolded her roundly for her apparent extravagance with the housekeeping money. Hannah listened in silence, face downcast, while he thundered on.

'This is what happens when I do not stand over you,' he roared finally. 'You take advantage of my trust in you to squander money away like water! Begone, you lazy slut, and send Mistress Topaz to me.'

Hannah told Topaz, 'I do not think his affairs with Frau Secker can be progressing favourably, for he is in an evil mood today. He wishes to see you, Topaz, but beware his tongue!'

Topaz stood dutifully before Kaspar, eyes meekly downcast and her hands folded, and waited for the tirade to begin. Instead, to her surprise, Kaspar walked round his desk and came to her.

'My child,' he said, and Topaz was surprised by the unwonted gentleness of his voice, 'I trust you are faring well. I regret I have been too preoccupied of late to be able to have much conversation with you, but let that not make you misunderstand my good intentions for you.'

Topaz was puzzled by his remarks, but had more discretion than to enquire his meaning. Presently he went on.

'You know I have always had your best interests at heart, do you not, Topaz?'

'Indeed, stepfather.'

'And so, at great inconvenience both to my time and my person, I have been busy while in Munich furthering your interests yet again.'

Kaspar waited for Topaz's reaction, but as she did not understand his meaning, she remained silent.

'I felt it was my duty to your mother—God rest her soul!' ——he broke off and hastily crossed himself, and Topaz did likewise—— 'to make it my business to see that all three of her daughters were well provided for.

'Perle and Saphir, as you know, are comfortably settled with good husbands and only you remain. For this reason I have been busy conducting negotiations to settle you equally comfortably with a home and husband of your own.'

He paused and looked expectantly at Topaz, but she was still looking floorwards.

'Well?' he said peevishly. 'Are you not grateful that I take so much trouble for you?'

'Yes, stepfather, thank you.'

Kaspar regarded her with surprise. 'Are you not curious, child, to know the name and station of the man I have selected as your husband-to-be?'

'It is a matter of indifference to me, stepfather.'

Kaspar's expression changed instantly from surprise to anger. 'Indifference, is it? I take the trouble to spend time I could have spent in Frau Secker's company, in doing the best I can for you, and you have the supreme insolence to tell me it is a matter of indifference to you! I sometimes wonder why I waste my time on you; I might just as well let the village idiot have you, for all the thanks you give me!'

He turned sharply and walked towards the window, breathing deeply in his anger. After a moment he turned to Topaz again.

'Well it is all arranged. At the end of the summer you will be formally betrothed to Herr Karl Winder, merchant of Cologne.'

Topaz heard his words as through a mist. 'Do you hear me Mistress Topaz?' she heard him say, but she could not reply. She could marry no man but Charles!

The rug on the floor before Kaspar's desk was beginning to dance a jig, and the more Topaz tried to concentrate on Kaspar's words, the more the rug danced. Finally she gave up the struggle to concentrate, and to try to hold the rug still, and slipped into a crumpled heap on the floor.

The bedchamber was hot and oppressive. Topaz opened her eyes. Hannah was just opening the door to let a gentleman out. After a few moments she returned.

'Who was that, Hannah?' Topaz asked her.

'The physician. Kaspar was so taken aback when you collapsed in his study, he thought he had occasioned it by the shock of his announcement to you, so he sent Hans for Doctor Leimann.'

Topaz's eyes opened wide in horror. 'Then it will all come out! Did the physician realize——?'

'Yes, my child,' said Hannah sadly. 'He saw at once. I fear he is telling Herr Kaspar at this moment of his findings.'

'Oh Hannah! What shall I do? Kaspar will kill me!' Topaz cried.

'Hush now, child! He'll not harm you, 'tis more than he dare! 'Tis more like he will flay the hide off me for letting it happen, and i' faith, I think it is no more than I deserve,' Hannah said softly.

'No, no, Hannah!' cried Topaz, rising from the bed and thrusting her feet into her mules. 'I won't let him harm you!

You are the only creature who has ever shown me love and kindness—except Charles, that is.'

'Charles!' Hannah snorted. 'A lot of kindness he showed! To seduce you then abandon you, is that kindness?'

'Hannah! I'll not have you speak of Charles thus! He loves me—he said so. He has no idea I am with child, or he would have come for me ere this, I know it!'

Topaz's face crumpled. She could not bear that anyone should malign her beloved Charles. He did love her—his eyes had been serious and honest as the day when he told her so.

The heavy oak door of the chamber suddenly burst open, and Kaspar strode in. His usually weatherbeaten face was tight-lipped and white with suppressed fury.

'Get out!' he said softly and venomously to Hannah. Hannah cast one look of abject fear at Topaz and fled. Topaz stood on the far side of the bed from Kaspar, watching him with huge eyes.

'Is it true?' Kaspar hissed.

'What, stepfather?' Topaz asked.

Kaspar growled and came round the bed to her, gripping her wrist viciously. 'That you let some fellow lay you and blow your belly up with child!' he roared, twisting her arm.

'No, no,' Topaz screamed as the pain ripped through her arm.

'No? When the physician tells me you are more than four months gone with child already? You're a liar as well as a whore! There's a special place reserved in hell for common bawds like you!' he roared, and threw Topaz on the bed.

Topaz whimpered and lay still for fear of further rousing his wrath. Kaspar paced the chamber, snorting and raging.

'To think of the time and energy I've wasted on you, you slut! To look at you, one would think butter wouldn't melt in your mouth! You had me utterly fooled. But what worthy merchant would consider you as a wife now, you soiled piece of goods? What a fool I shall appear when I have to retract from the agreement I made with Herr Winder—it will probably cost me a pretty penny too! Did you think of that, you trollop, before you gave yourself to your swain?'

'I did not know of your transaction, stepfather,' Topaz wept.

'What difference does that make? You had no right to give freely of your favours to some village dolt without the benefit of wedlock. And you with such pious airs too!'

Topaz sobbed softly and Kaspar still paced up and down. Finally he stopped in front of her.

'Who is he? Who is the man who is responsible? I insist that he marries you at once, so that at least the child shall be born in wedlock.'

Topaz sobbed louder.

'Who is he, I say?' Kaspar demanded, coming to the bed-post and leaning threateningly over her.

'His name is . . . Charles Barlow.' Topaz's words were indistinct.

'What's that you say? Barlow? That's a foreign name.'

'He was an Englishman, passing this way on his journey to Rotterdam. Oh stepfather, please! I know he'll come back and marry me! He loves me—he said so!'

Kaspar's face registered disbelief and horror. 'An Englishman? A filthy foreigner! And you believed him when he said he loved you?' Kaspar laughed sardonically. 'Every man says that in order to get his way with a woman, and you were fool enough to fall for his smoothness. Your filthy animal instincts were too much for you, my girl. You're no better than an animal in the fields!'

In disgust Kaspar turned away from her. He stood in silence for a few moments, gazing out of the window, then he spoke, his back still turned towards her.

'I want no foreign bastards in this house,' he said coldly, his voice glittering with determination. 'I have proposed marriage to Frau Secker, and she is at the moment considering my proposal. She was quite impressed with what she saw of Torwald, and I have no intention that you should ruin my prospects of marriage by giving birth to the products of your whoring here.'

He paused. Topaz lay fearful, wondering what he proposed to do with her.

'Therefore I shall enquire at the nunnery at Niemandsheim whether the Mother Abbess there will consider you as novice —after you have discarded your burden,' he added.

'But my babe—what will happen to my child?' Topaz whispered.

Kaspar turned to her. 'I'll warrant the nuns will place him in an orphanage for you, you need not fret.'

'But I shall not see him again!'

'What need has a nun of a child? 'Twill be a fitting penance for you to relinquish it.'

'No, no, stepfather! He is Charles' child too, and I love Charles with all my heart. I will not give up his child!'

Kaspar's voice was icy with anger. 'Do you dare to defy me, after all I have done for you? Even now, ungrateful as you are, you throw my attempts to help you back into my face.'

'Charles will come back,' Topaz moaned.

'You are a fool to believe it,' snapped Kaspar. 'You have seen the last of that lechering young man, I'll warrant you.'

'He promised we should meet again,' Topaz said.

'In the corner of hell kept for fornicators, that's where you'll see him again. However mistress, I leave you to think on my words. In the morning you will tell me of your decision to enter the nunnery, then I shall go to see Mother Abbess.'

Kaspar turned abruptly and left Topaz to weep in utter misery.

'How does the affair with the Princess Henrietta progress?' James asked Charles one sultry evening as they walked along a country lane.

Charles shrugged his shoulders. 'Oh, she seems pleased with my attentions, but oh James! Have you seen her skin and teeth at close quarters? It seems a high price to pay for the sake of small change. However, Henrietta thinks her mother may put up some opposition to our courtship; since I'm penniless and commonly called Charles Lackland, no one holds me in very high esteem as a prospective son-in-law, I fear.'

James chuckled. 'If you can win over the daughter with your charm, the mother will soon fall victim too, I'll be bound.'

'I would I had your confidence,' Charles retorted. 'But stay though,' he added, his eyes suddenly taking on a gleam, 'I did gain something from my visits to Henrietta. She has the pertest, prettiest little wench I've ever laid eyes on for a chambermaid. A slender, dark-haired little maid, with the most mischievous, teasing blue eyes.

'I couldn't take my eyes off her all evening, and she knew it, the little hussy. She led me a right merry dance in the shrubbery after supper. But for the untimely arrival of my valet, I'd have had her. But I'll have her yet, damme if I don't.'

In the morning Kaspar sent Hannah to fetch Topaz to his study.

'Well, mistress? Have you thought over my proposal?' he said gruffly. He was seated behind his desk, pen in hand.

Topaz stood silent.

'Come now,' said Kaspar with exasperation, 'I must have your answer! Will you enter Niemandsheim as I suggest?'

Still Topaz did not reply. Her brain was numb. The only thought she was capable of, was that entering the nunnery meant giving up the child which was now beginning to move within her. Charles would not approve of her surrendering their child, she felt sure. Not for one moment did she doubt that they would meet again, but he would never be able to find her in a nunnery.

Finally she spoke. 'No, stepfather,' she said. The words were so faint that Kaspar barely heard her.

'What's that?'

'No, stepfather,' she repeated, more firmly this time.

Kaspar's fingers clenched on the quill pen in his hand, and Topaz saw his knuckles whiten.

'Now listen to me, mistress. Do you know what the punishment is for the mother of a bastard child?' Topaz shook her head slowly. Kaspar leaned forward. 'She is led through the streets naked,' he hissed, 'and whipped till her flesh hangs in shreds. I will not have that happen to you! Do you think I want people to point the finger of derision at me?

'I shall have you out of this house one way or another, for I do not want you here when Frau Secker comes again. You yourself have destroyed your chance of marrying comfortably, and now you have only one choice left—to enter the nunnery as I advise, or to get out and make your own way in the world. Now choose!'

There was a pause when not a sound could be heard, then Topaz said quietly:

'Stepfather, I have never flouted your authority before, but in this I must do as my conscience dictates. I will not enter the nunnery.'

Kaspar's face muscles tightened and his coarse skin was scarlet.

'Then you choose to go your own way?'

'I must.'

'Then mistress, take what you can carry and leave this house this very day. I can tolerate such sinfulness under my roof no longer.'

In silence, Topaz turned and left the study.

In her chamber she sadly gathered together a few clothes, her rosary and what little money she had. She wrapped them all in a bundle then went in search of Hannah.

She searched the kitchen, the cellars, the house upstairs and down, then finally the stables and outhouses, but Hannah was nowhere to be found. Hans had seen no sign of her either since she had fetched Topaz to Kaspar's study.

'Tis passing strange, thought Topaz. She would have expected Hannah to be waiting outside the study when Topaz emerged, anxious to know the outcome of the interview with Kaspar. The only explanation she could make to herself was that Kaspar had sent Hannah from the house on some errand.

Sadly Topaz re-entered the house. She paused outside the oratory, and on impulse went in and knelt before the altar.

'St. Teresa, hearken to my prayer yet again!' she murmured. 'Once before you listened—and answered me. Listen to me now, I pray, and take care of those who are in need. Intercede for Kaspar too, to soften his heart and bring him peace, for he is an unhappy man. Bless Hannah and protect her from Kaspar's wrath, and lastly, bless me and my babe now that we are about to set forth into the world alone and unprotected.

'Guide my footsteps to Charles—this above all I pray. Lead me to where I may see my love again!'

Topaz left the oratory, picked up her bundle, and walked slowly towards the door. There she hesitated. No, there was no point in bidding Kaspar adieu, for he had already bid her begone.

She went out of the gate, and turned towards the Dutch border. That was the way Charles had gone when he left Torwald nearly five months ago.

'James! The Dowager's changed her mind about me.' Charles was jubilant. 'I wrote Henrietta a formal proposal of marriage. She fainted with happiness when she read it, I've been told. The old girl's playing for time though—she wants time to consider, she says, but the hare's in the trap, I think! If you see my brother Henry, tell him the good news, will you?'

But Charles' jubilation was premature. The army's sudden domination in England caused the Dowager to have second thoughts, and Henrietta was obliged to reject her suitor. Charles was forced to content himself with Henrietta's amorous chambermaid for a night or two.

FIVE

ALL day Topaz trudged the country lanes towards the border. When night fell she was still deep in the countryside, and she thanked Heaven for the fine weather when she was obliged to sleep under a hedgerow.

Next day the weather was still hot and the still, sultry air soon made her feel tired and footsore. The heat hung in a heavy haze across the daisy-spattered fields, and by evening Topaz was weak and faint from hunger. Berries picked from the hedges and water from a stream was no sustenance for a woman with many miles to go.

Towards nightfall she saw a low thatched cottage, spruce in its new coat of whitewash. Thank heaven! Maybe here she could find much-needed rest and food.

She approached timidly. A child and a dog came running out to meet her.

'Is your mother about?' Topaz asked the child, a little boy about four or five years old. The dog was sniffing at her skirts curiously. The boy looked up at Topaz with huge, trusting eyes.

'Are you the midwife? My father's been gone ages looking for you,' the child said reproachfully.

'The midwife? No, not I.' The child's expression drooped. 'Where is your mother?' Topaz asked again.

'She's in bed. I haven't had my supper yet,' the boy replied.

Topaz felt bewildered. 'Is your mother ill? Has she—is she going to have a baby? she asked, fearful of the reply. She felt weak with exhaustion, and her knowledge of childbirth was limited to the little Hannah had told her.

The boy snorted. 'She's got it. Last night Papa sent me to sleep in the stable. He stayed with Mama, and they got the babe this morning. Then Papa rode to seek the midwife again, and bid me take care of Mama till he returned. I thought you were the midwife.'

'Why has he gone for her now?' Topaz asked him.

'I don't know. Because Mama is ill, I think.'

'I see.' She paused, then added, 'Would you like me to get you something ready to eat? If your mother will allow me, that is.'

The boy's face lit up. 'Would you? Oh, yes please!'

He turned and entered the cottage, and Topaz followed him in. 'Mama,' he said, 'Here's a lady says she will make me my supper.'

Topaz heard a low moan from a truckle bed in the corner of the low-ceilinged room. She crossed to the bed.

A young woman, her face almost translucent in its pallor, lay in the bed, her brow covered in perspiration and her fair hair straggling all over the pillow. In the crook of her arm lay a tiny, redhaired infant, peacefully asleep.

'Good even, mistress,' said Topaz. 'I hope you will forgive my intrusion.'

The girl opened her eyes and gazed at Topaz without interest.

'How long has your husband been gone?' Topaz asked her.

'Since about midday.'

'Have you eaten since then?'

The girl shook her head slowly. 'There's salt beef and cheese and ale—help yourself and give Karl to eat,' she murmured.

Karl, the German name for Charles, thought Topaz, and in spite of her weariness she smiled. It was a good omen at the start of her journey to find Charles.

She put down her bundle and cloak and hacked a piece of beef from the carcase hanging from a hook in the ceiling. She put more wood on the fire and the beef in a pan over it to boil. Then she cut a wedge of cheese for Karl and gave him a mug of milk and some bread, and he ate hungrily.

'Can I give you cheese also?' she asked the girl in the bed.

The girl groaned. 'Thank you, no. Water, please.'

Topaz poured water from an earthenware jug on the table and took it to her. The girl tried to lift her head, but was too weak.

Topaz moved the sleeping baby, then slid her arm under the girl's shoulders and lifted her. The girl gulped the water down, then lay back and licked her lips. She smiled a weak smile of gratitude. 'Who are you?' she asked. 'A traveller, or a pedlar or gipsy?'

Topaz smiled and shook her head. 'A traveller—my name is Topaz Birke. I was coming to the house to ask for a night's shelter, before I knew you were sick,' she said.

'You must stay,' the girl said.

'I can pay you,' Topaz said. 'I have a little money.'

'No, please, as a kindness to me—take care of Karl for me—at least until Detlev returns.'

Topaz felt sorry for the poor sick girl, her eyes wide with pleading and her face soaked in perspiration. She poured more water into a bowl and bathed the girl's forehead, then smoothed her pillow. The baby woke, screwed up its face and began to howl. A tender look came over the girl's face as she put the baby to her breast and gently kissed the down on top of its head.

Topaz smiled as she seated herself in a chair by the window and watched them. Karl, she saw, had fallen asleep on the hearth, and in the silence, broken only by the hissing and bubbling of the pot on the fire, Topaz too soon slept from exhaustion.

Charles looked up from struggling into his hose as James entered his bedchamber. James looked serious.

'Is there news from England?' Charles asked him.

James nodded. 'The balance of power between the Army and the Parliament is still an uneasy one. The Army is growing more restless and ill-disciplined, and there are rumours some of the junior officers are in favour of mutiny.'

Charles straightened up. 'Do you think it could be true?'

James shrugged. 'It's possible. And I think the people are heartily sick of military rule too.'

Charles reflected. 'It might be a wise move to write to General Monk. He is still in Scotland, watching what goes on, and I think he cares little for Fleetwood's rotten army and its rule over England. Do you think he might declare for monarchy if I were to approach him?'

'Monk is a cautious man,' James replied. 'His army is small compared to Fleetwood's but it is well-disciplined and his careful administration means he has ample funds to pay his troops. Yes, I think it might well prove worth while.'

'I shall write to him tonight,' said Charles.

Topaz was jerked out of her dream by the dull clatter of hoofbeats coming to a rapid halt at the cottage door. The door burst open and a short, stocky, darkhaired young man strode in.

'Come mistress, quickly!' he called, and a middle-aged woman bustled in after him. The young man glanced curiously at Topaz then crossed immediately to the bed.

'Grete, my dear,' he said in a low, urgent voice. 'How fare you now, my little one? I have brought the midwife now, but I fear it took me hours to find her.'

The girl, Topaz could see from where she sat, smiled weakly at her husband. The midwife pushed him briskly out of her way.

'It grows dusk,' she said curtly. 'Bring me light.'

The young man crossed to the hearth, stepping over his sleeping son, and lit a lantern with a taper. He placed the lantern on a chest beside the bed, and stood by while the midwife rolled up her sleeves and looked carefully at the girl.

'Mmmm,' she said as she felt her brow. Then she removed the sleeping babe and looked for somewhere to place it. Seeing Topaz, she crossed to her and dumped the child in her lap. Then she returned to the girl and whipped the covers off her. Topaz gasped as she saw that the girl lay in a welter of blood.

The girl groaned and stirred. 'It's cold, so cold,' she moaned.

'Hot schnapps,' the woman snapped. 'Schnapps and hot water.'

The man nodded, bewildered, and blundered to the table. He poured water into a skillet and took it to the fire.

'Let me do that.' Topaz came to life at last. She placed the babe carefully on the bedcovers lying on the floor, and crossed to take the skillet from the man. He let her go without a word, then went and poured brandy into a tankard.

The woman was soaking sheets in the bowl of water Topaz had left on the table. After some minutes' work she turned to the young husband. 'I think we have staunched the bleeding now,' she said, 'but the girl has a high fever and must be nursed carefully. It is the fever of childbed and mayhap will last some time.'

Topaz was pouring the water into the schnapps. The midwife took the tankard from her and returned to the sick woman. For the first time the young husband really took note of Topaz. Now she felt was the time to explain her presence; up to now both he and the midwife had been too preoccupied with more serious matters.

'And as I am in no great haste,' she concluded, 'I should be glad to stay a day or two and care for your wife.'

The young man considered her thoughtfully then nodded. 'Mistress, you would be welcome in any event,' he said quietly, 'but now especially, when my wife is sick and I am obliged to work from morn till dusk gathering my crops. I should be greatly obliged to you if you would stay.'

The midwife had finished her work. 'She will sleep now,' she said as she straightened up. 'When she wakes she must be given good nourishment—hot broths, milk possets, to help her regain the strength she has lost. I shall give you a potion to help reduce the fever, but she is but a fragile creature and must be nursed with great care.'

Topaz listened to her instructions carefully, but already fatigue was causing her brain to mist over. It was with the utmost gratitude to St. Teresa that she finally sank on the straw pallet Herr Detlev showed her in a tiny adjoining chamber, and fell soundly asleep.

At cockcrow Detlev roused her. 'I must away to the four-acre field to begin gathering the corn,' he said. 'Grete still has a fever but the bleeding has not begun again. If you should need me, send Karl down to me,' and he set off with the cart and his broad-shouldered plough-horse.

The succeeding days followed the same pattern; Detlev set off at dawn and returned at dusk, and Topaz cared for the sick Grete and Karl with gentle care. Gradually Grete's fever abated and the harassed look of worry began to fade from Detlev's dark, suntanned face.

'I fear she has not the strength for child bearing,' he murmured one evening as he sat, content after his evening meal, by the fire. He sounded almost irritated, Topaz thought to herself, and the thought was confirmed by his next statement.

'She is too small-boned and delicate to give birth easily. When she had Karl it took her three days to bring him forth. My father was right after all when he bid me marry a well-built, full-blown country girl, but I loved Grete, and when the blood is young and eager. . . .' His voice tailed away, full of regret.

Topaz looked across at the pale, tousled girl asleep in the bed and felt anger welling up inside her. 'She has borne you a healthy son, and now a daughter,' she pointed out resentfully.

'That is so,' he nodded slowly, 'but she is ill for weeks after, and on a farm every hand counts. When she cannot work, I must pay someone to care for her, and there is no one to help me in the fields.'

Topaz was furious. He wanted Grete both to bear his children and to labour in the fields like a man, and felt cheated when childbirth sapped her strength. In her pity for the girl, Topaz resolved to offer her own services.

'You work in the fields?' Detlev looked at her in amazement, his eyes running up and down her figure. Topaz felt embarrassed and coloured hotly. 'You are even slighter than she!' he said, and began to chuckle. Topaz felt conscious of the thickening that was beginning to swell below her waist, but he was evidently unaware of it; however, she saw to her confusion that his eyes were lingering on her high, rounded breasts. She turned away quickly.

'At least I can bring you food in the fields at midday,' she said quietly.

'As you wish, mistress,' he answered curtly, and went out to water his horse.

The weeks passed. Topaz grew almost content with her life on the farm. For the first time she could remember she was needed and it was wonderful to feel she had a purpose—to care for the family and restore Grete to health. The gentle girl was full of love and gratitude for the kindly stranger who tempted her appetite with novel dishes and cared for her husband and child so ably. Topaz inwardly blessed Hannah for teaching her the culinary skills which now were proving so useful. Gradually Grete began to move, though weakly, about the house again.

There was only one flaw in the smoothness of life. Topaz's babe was growing and thriving unseen, and Hannah had said it would probably be born in the new year or early spring. Already it was September. If Topaz was to find Charles before their child was born, she would have to move on soon.

The crops were at last safely stored in the granary, and Detlev had managed to secure help to begin the haymaking. At midday Topaz took him cheese and bread and fruit in a basket, and a jug of ale. It was a hot, heavy day, and she stood at the edge of the field and watched his muscular, bare brown body, clad only in ragged hose, rising and dipping rhythmically with the scythe. There was no doubt he was a hardworking man, and she yearned for the day she and Charles would be together thus.

She set the basket down and slipped the shoulders of her gown further down. In this heat the cloth was wellnigh unbearable on the skin. Detlev looked up and saw her, smiled, and came leisurely across to her.

'The country air suits you, mistress Topaz,' he said, his teeth gleaming against the burnished glow of his skin. 'There is a comely bloom on your skin that was not there when you first came hither.'

The frank look of admiration in his eyes made Topaz catch her breath. It was exactly the look she had seen so often in Charles' eyes that magical week—was it already five months ago? She must speak to Detlev about leaving and moving on, now that Grete was so much improved.

She bent to unpack the food from the cloth in the basket, and on straightening up she saw his eyes were gleaming, watching the rise of her bosom from her gown. She pulled the shoulders of the gown higher again, and Detlev turned his attention to the food.

He devoured it hungrily, then lay back on the grass. 'Thunder clouds over there,' he remarked. He was right. The still, intense heat of the day gave way to an eerie yellowish light and an atmosphere of highly-charged tension. The other workers in the field one by one waved and disappeared.

'We'd best return home before the storm breaks,' Detlev said, picking up the scythe and basket, and he and Topaz walked quickly towards the house. By the time they reached the copse a half mile away, heavy rainspots were falling fast, and when they were within sight of the barn the heavens suddenly opened up and spat fire. An almighty crash of thunder ripped the clouds apart and the couple were suddenly deluged.

'Into the barn, quick!' Detlev shouted above the roar, and Topaz picked up her soaking skirts and ran after him. They reached the shelter of the barn, panting and breathless, and Detlev threw himself down on the hay. Topaz leaned against the door jamb, gasping for breath.

Detlev was lying back on one elbow. Rivulets of rain trickled from his wiry dark hair and ran down his brawny shoulders. He shook himself like a terrier, then leaned back again, watching her, an amused smile twitching the corners of his mouth.

'Come, sit awhile till the storm abates,' he invited her. She lowered herself on the hay a little way from him, and unbound her hair which was beginning to fall loose from the combs under the weight of the rain. The tresses fell heavily across her shoulders. Detlev's eyes shone dully in the yellow gloom. He slid across to where she sat.

At this close range she could smell the cool freshness of the rain on his body mingled with the sickly pungency of his sweat. She averted her face quickly, and in doing so her hair swept clingingly across his face. He raised a work-roughened hand to turn her face back again, and she saw again the admiring look in his eyes. His hand dropped to her shoulder and he drew her closer, his eyes half closing. Topaz tried to break away, but he firmly pushed her back.

'Forgive me, but you are so lovely, mistress,' he murmured. ' 'Tis more than a man can bear, to have your sweet-scented body so close. And I am a man who has been long denied.' His eyes had a heavy-lidded, slumbrous look about them as he hung over her. His hand slipped slowly down from her shoulders and covered her breast, then travelled on down.

Topaz fought to shake him off, and she saw his eyes flicker open, then stare in amazement, his hand on her stomach. The surprise in his eyes was slowly replaced by a smile.

'Why, mistress Topaz!' he exclaimed, smiling broadly now. 'I thought to have been the first man to tumble you, but now I see you are no stranger to the sport!'

Detlev sat up, laughing loudly, and let her go loose while he wiped a tear from his eye. Topaz sat up, furious. 'All these weeks,' he went on, his voice choking with laughter, 'All these weeks I thought you a pure and virtuous maid, such a beguiling look of innocence you wear, and all the time you are half gone with child! Is that why you were on the road, Topaz? Driven out of your parish for your whoring? Bringing a bastard child into the world which the parish refused to support?

'Come now, you can hardly refuse a man so long denied, after being my guest for so long.' He reached for her again, tears of laughter trickling down his begrimed cheek.

Topaz, aflame with anger, waited to hear no more. She picked up her skirts and ran out into the storm, leaving Detlev still helpless with laughter.

In the cottage Grete was sitting on the bed, singing to the frightened Karl who lay huddled under the bedcovers. She did not hear Topaz creep in, collect her bundle of belongings and steal out into the storm again. Topaz set off, with heavy heart, on the road towards the coast.

'Oh my darling,' she murmured to herself, 'I am coming to you now. St. Teresa, guide my footsteps. . . .'

'Have you had a reply from General Monk, Charles?' James enquired.

Charles shook his head gloomily. 'I made approach to him, first through Sir John Grenville, then through his brother, the Rev. Nicholas Monk, but not a word has he replied.'

James considered the buckle on his shoe thoughtfully. 'Well, as I said, he's a cautious man, and not likely to declare for monarchy till the moment is ripe. He makes no secret of his preference for lawful constitution in place of power-grabbers, but no doubt he is biding his time. At least he has not refused you.'

Charles nodded, then stretched luxuriously. 'At any rate there is a silver lining to the clouds of gloom. King Louis is to be betrothed to the Spanish Infanta, and while he is away I shall take the opportunity to visit Minette at Colombes. Do you know it is six years since I saw my little sister? She was only nine then, and I wonder whether I shall recognize her now; girls change so much as they grow up.'

He gazed at the ceiling, lost in memory, for a few moments before continuing. 'Poor Minette, she has not had an easy life either, but she was always so gentle and kind. You know, James, of all the women in the world, Minette is the rarest, and I love her dearly. Truly love her, I mean. Other women may hold my heart for a moment, but little Minette holds my heart and my soul for ever.'

James smiled at the unwonted tenderness in Charles' voice. 'To other, more mundane matters though, Charles. There is a loyal subject of yours lately arrived from England, one Roger Palmer, who has been of invaluable help in keeping us informed of the situation in Wales. He is waiting below to be presented to Your Majesty.

'An honest, unpretentious enough fellow,' James added with a mischievous smile, 'but I think you may find his pretty wife an interesting eyeful.'

Without a word Charles rose and took James' arm and led him from the chamber.

SIX

TOPAZ walked blindly on, head lowered against the slashing rain, until the storm died almost as suddenly as it had been born. With the fickle temperament of a courted beauty the sun decided to shine again, and gradually as she walked Topaz's sodden clothes dried out on her back. Only the squelch in her shoes remained to remind her of the storm and its consequences in the barn.

Towards evening as the sun was beginning to dip lower, a heavy farm cart laden with vegetables trundled slowly out of a side lane on to the road she was walking. An elderly farmer sat on the box, his hat pulled low over his bushy eyebrows.

'Whither are you bound, lass?' he asked gruffly. 'I'm for Hoogstraeten, to the market. Hop up, if you've a mind.'

Hoogstraeten, Topaz knew, was a town on the border, well on her way to Rotterdam. She nodded her thanks and climbed up beside him. He eyed her quizzically but spoke little. She knew he was wondering why she was abroad alone, and felt it best to offer some explanation, and murmured vaguely about going to join her husband in Hoogstraeten for market day.

He whipped up the bedraggled horse to a trot, and by nightfall Topaz could feel the cobblestones of the town causing the cart to jolt and shake its load about dangerously. The farmer set her down at an inn and drove on to the market place.

Sounds of laughter and riotous singing came from the open windows of the inn. A couple of pretty wenches stood framed in the light of the doorway, and they laughed and nudged each other in the ribs as Topaz passed them to enter. A couple of men sitting at the trestle tables set down their tankards and turned admiringly to watch her approach the innkeeper.

'Is she the latest addition to the attractions of the Nimble Rabbit?' called one of them. The innkeeper frowned, then smiled broadly at Topaz. She hoped she had sufficient money to pay for a room for the night.

'What is the cost of a night's lodging?' she asked him timidly.

'Ten marks, fräulein,' he replied.

Topaz gasped in astonishment. At Torwald ten marks would have bought food for a week. She counted the coins in her pocket again.

'I regret I have only five marks,' she told him. 'Have you a cheaper room?'

There was laughter all round her. Topaz felt sick with embarrassment.

'I'll give thee a night's lodging, lass, any time,' a raucous voice called.

'Or I either,' called another.

The innkeeper turned on them. 'Gentlemen, this lady is a visitor. I'll thank you to be civil to her,' he said crisply, then turned to her again. 'It's market week here,' he said, 'and every inn is fully charged with visitors, but I'll find you a room,' he added when he saw Topaz's dismayed look.

He led her upstairs to a small garret with a truckle bed. ' 'Tis no palace chamber, but the best I can do.'

'Thank you sir, you are most kind,' Topaz murmured.

He left her and returned shortly with cold beef and some pasty on a platter, and some canary wine. Topaz could see he was eyeing her with some curiosity.

Eventually he spoke. 'Mistress,' he said quietly, 'If you would pardon my impertinence, it would appear that you are short of money. If you cared to, you could find work here to earn more.'

Topaz's interest was aroused at once. Time was limited but to have money would make travelling and finding Charles so much easier. 'What kind of work?' she asked.

'Helping me with the work of the inn,' he answered. 'Serve the gentlemen with ale and food, keep them laughing and merry so they call for more ale.'

Topaz considered. It did not appeal to her to mix with those rough fellows below, but the work did not sound too hard, and money was essential to her.

'How much will you pay me?' she asked.

'Five marks a week, your board and lodging. And probably the customers will tip you if you serve them well,' he answered.

'Agreed,' Topaz said decisively, and with a smile the innkeeper left her.

Charles clapped James heartily on the shoulder. 'By Jupiter, but you were right about that Palmer woman! Isn't she a glorious armful? What a superb figure, and an arrogant toss of the head that would tempt the Pope himself! And such eyes. A man could drown in those violet-blue depths. How old is she, James? What is her name?'

James laughed softly at Charles' enthusiasm. 'She is nineteen, and her name is Barbara.'

'Barbara, eh?' Charles rolled the name slowly off his tongue. 'And she looks as if she could be a little barbarian too!' He laughed loudly at his joke. James nodded knowingly.

'Indeed, she is known to be somewhat wild,' he said carefully.

Charles' eye gleamed. 'No regard for the vows of matrimony, eh?'

'Precious little. She chased young Chesterfield and was his lover from the time she was fifteen till she married at eighteen, then she and Anne Hamilton kept house together on Ludgate Hill for some time to take all their fancies to. She leads poor Roger Palmer a right merry dance, and the poor fool is so besotted with her he turns a blind eye to it all.'

'Why is she here with him in Breda then?'

'It seems Mistress Palmer has lately been ill—of the pox it is said—so mayhap she is abroad for her health.'

'The pox? I saw not a mark on her glorious skin of the pox.' Charles paused and reflected, his eyes dancing with excitement. 'But I promise you one thing, James, if there is a pockmark anywhere on her body, I swear I shall find it, and that right soon too, or my name is not Charles Stuart.'

Topaz awoke to a stale, musty smell. She rose and dressed in her black gown, the ragged, dirty kirtle of which bore evidence to her long journey. Through the cracks in the floorboards of her chamber she could catch glimpses of the taproom below, and she realized it was the stench of old ale that rose and seeped upwards. She shuddered. 'Twas a foul lodging, but better by far than sleeping under the hedgerows now autumn was here.

She descended the rickety staircase to the kitchen below. A tall, red-haired girl, full and shapely, was gathering up and washing pots and tankards. She nodded briefly to Topaz, yawned, and indicated a pan of gruel on the hob.

'Help yourself,' she said, cluttering the dishes into a bowl of greasy water. 'You're the new wench, are you not?'

Topaz nodded as she spooned up the thin gruel. 'Then you can help the others tidy and sweep when you are done. What is your name, girl?'

'Topaz.'

The girl paused in her washing, then grinned. 'I see. A new fancy name to suit your work, is it? Have no fear, I shall not question your real name. Mine is Klara, and I am the chief of the girls here. They all obey my instructions. Is that clear?'

Topaz nodded again. Why should Klara think she was lying, hiding her real name? No matter. Klara gave her a hunk of bread and some cold beef, and Topaz ate hungrily.

'Now to work,' said Klara when she had finished eating. She surveyed Topaz critically up and down. 'That gown will pass for the kitchen work,' she pronounced at length, 'but you must have something better to wear for serving in the tavern. Come, I will see what we can find.'

Obediently Topaz followed her upstairs again. Klara led her to her chamber, somewhat larger than Topaz's own, but almost filled by the enormous tester bed in the centre. Klara edged her way round it to a trunk by the window, the lid of which she threw open. Handfuls of gowns and scarves she pulled out and threw on the bed, glancing from each one to Topaz and clicking her tongue impatiently.

Suddenly her eyes lit up. She pounced on an emerald green silk gown and turned to Topaz with a radiant smile. 'This is the one,' she beamed, and held it up against Topaz.

Topaz was overawed by its beauty. The deep green was beautifully set off by rows of silver lace on the lowcut bodice and looped on the skirts.

'Try it on,' Klara commanded. Topaz slid off her own filthy gown, wondering why Klara should be so concerned about her appearance. Perhaps her ragged state would not attract sufficient custom, and Klara's earnings would suffer.

'Beautiful,' Klara murmured as she helped her smooth out the skirt. Topaz shuddered at the amount of her bosom that protruded above the silver lace, and tried to pull the bodice higher.

'No, no.' Klara snatched her hand away and smoothed the bodice down again. 'You fill the gown admirably, child. You'll have no difficulty in gaining clients. Are you new to this work, Topaz?'

Topaz nodded again. She felt dumbstruck before this lovely, lively girl. 'Have no fear, you will do well. The men prefer little-used goods,' Klara said cryptically.

Topaz sneezed. Klara looked at her with concern, and Topaz felt her eyes stinging and she shivered. 'Are you ill, girl?' Klara demanded.

'A touch of the ague, I think. I was soaked to the skin yesterday. Might I perhaps wear a shawl over my shoulders? I am so cold.'

Klara hesitated, then nodded. She rummaged through the trunk again and produced a fine white woollen shawl, shot through with silver threads. 'This I think will match your gown,' she said, folding it over Topaz's shoulders.

Gratefully Topaz snuggled into its warmth. She was glad to cover her bosom, revealed almost to the nipples.

'Just for a day or two, mind,' Klara warned. 'It will not do to conceal the wares too long or Herr Franz will start to complain. In any event, I shall need it myself ere long, now the chilly evenings are drawing in.'

Topaz smiled her thanks, but inwardly felt a little puzzled and suspicious. The clothes Klara had given her were far too fine for merely serving ale in the tavern, and her comments about concealing the wares, and the men preferring little-used goods caused Topaz to suspect Franz's intentions as to the nature of her work at the inn.

She smiled ruefully to herself. Before leaving Torwald such uncharitable suspicions would never have entered her mind. She resolved not to prejudge Franz but wait and see.

Before noon customers began to arrive at the tavern, calling loudly for food and ale. Franz cast an approving look at Topaz's appearance and set her to drawing ale and hurrying backwards and forwards with the foaming tankards. Klara was not to be seen, but the two pretty girls Topaz had seen at the inn door the previous night dashed busily to and from the kitchen with heavily laden platters of food for the hungry farmers.

Topaz winced when she heard the men's raucous laughter as one of them dealt the dark-haired wench a resounding thwack on her plump bottom as she leaned across the table, then followed it with a pinch that made her squeal like a piglet. The man, a big, piratical fellow with a bushy black beard, roared with laughter. 'I'll be busy dealing with my own hogs in the market this afternoon,' he bellowed to the girl's retreating figure, 'but I'll be back to ring your nose for you this evening, little one.'

Franz smiled contentedly and served the group with more ale. Topaz felt hot and dizzy despite the coolness of the day, and her eyes still stung and her throat ached. She was filled with revulsion for these coarse men, and wished she could go to her chamber for a time and lie down.

Gradually the crowd thinned and dispersed, for the afternoon market was in full swing again. Topaz took the empty tankards to the kitchen where the other two girls were busy washing and stacking the platters. Franz followed her in.

'Lisa,' he said to the dark wench, 'see to it that your chamber is neat and sweet smelling before the evening. The stench in there would drive even the most undiscerning customer away.'

The girl pouted and continued washing the dishes. When Franz left the kitchen she turned to the other girl. 'Chamber, he says, garret more like,' she snapped. 'There's barely room to swing a cat in there, let alone. . . .' She stopped suddenly as the other girl nudged her sharply. 'What is it?'

The other girl nodded towards Topaz. 'Oh, her! Well you don't think she doesn't know, surely?' She surveyed Topaz curiously a moment, then smiled widely. 'I think mayhap you're right, Hilde. She does look the little innocent, does she not?'

Lisa dried her hands then stood, hands on hips. 'Well then, you have much still to learn, mistress,' she said mockingly. 'You're a pretty enough piece and no doubt will attract attention easily enough, but let me give you a piece of good advice, my girl. Whatever price Franz demands for your services, tell him you want half. He'll offer a quarter, but for wares that fetch custom readily he'll agree to a half if you're persuasive.

'Just one thing, though. Do not poach on my field or Hilde's. And if you dare to try to take Klara's customers, she'll have your eyes out in a second. So don't say we haven't warned you.' She turned to Hilde with a satisfied smile of having done her duty.

Topaz felt sick. It was clear enough now what her work in the 'Nimble Rabbit' was to be. 'Keep the customers contented,' Franz had said, but he had not revealed in what way she was to keep them happy. And she had been foolish enough to think he was a kind man.

Disillusioned and sick at heart, Topaz felt utterly desolate and in despair. In the slack trade of the afternoon she was able to lie down on her pallet and think confused, tortured thoughts. How was she to travel on and find Charles without money? The only means to gaining money was to agree to Franz's proposals, but the prospect of allowing those coarse, revolting men to paw her and have their way with her made her gorge rise. This was so different from the pure, blissful, idyllic love she and Charles had shared, and debased the very coin of love.

No, no! she cried inwardly, I cannot do it! But what am I to do for the best, for Charles and his babe that I nurture under my heart? Oh St. Teresa! You have never failed me in the past, guide me now, I pray, and show me what I am to do!

Topaz fell into a fitful sleep, with agonizing nightmares of huge, hairy beasts hovering over her supine figure, and awoke sweating and half-mad with terror. Low voices were deep in conversation outside her door.

'But why can she not come?' she heard Franz say vehemently. 'The taproom is bursting with customers roaring for service. She must come!'

'It is no use,' she heard Klara's voice reply curtly. 'The girls are under my supervision as you agreed. This one is not fit for service tonight. In any event, it may whet their appetites to keep them waiting, and you can charge so much more when she is available.'

Franz grunted, then asked, 'What ails the girl, anyway? I cannot afford to feed her long if she does not earn her keep.'

'An ague, that is all, I think. She was soaked to the marrow before she came hither, but now she has a high fever and is delirious. Have patience, 'twill not be long, a day or two at the most. Then she will work doubly hard to make up for it, I shall see to that.'

Franz murmured his reluctant agreement, and their footsteps faded down the corridor to the stairway. Topaz felt the room vibrating, and knew not whether it was the throbbing in her head or the roar of the customers in the taproom below. Nor did she care. She felt only utter relief that for the time being at least she was spared the agony of decision.

'For this relief, my thanks, St. Teresa,' she murmured before falling asleep again. Several times she awoke to hear the noisy creaking of the bed in the next chamber, and its significance caused her nightmares of devouring beasts to start anew.

James beckoned Charles away from the noisy, chattering group in the palace corridor. Charles, seeing the air of suppressed excitement about his big, powerful frame, excused himself and hurried to join him.

'What is it?' he asked curiously.

'General Monk has agreed with Lord Fairfax in Yorkshire to take action jointly to overthrow the Army,' James said excitedly. 'They have not yet openly declared for monarchy, but want to recall a full and free Parliament. Their intention is clear.'

Charles was gazing at him with wide eyes. A sudden look of anticipation leapt into them. 'Lord Thomas Fairfax?' he said. 'He is a man of great honour and integrity, and had no part in the killing of my father. What is more, he has great power. He and Monk between them should be able to achieve anything.'

'Indeed. The moment of restoration may be nearer than we thought or hoped for, Charles,' James said.

Charles nodded thoughtfully. 'You would be wise,' James went on, 'to act discreetly in the meantime, my friend, while England considers whether to restore you to your throne.'

'How do you mean?'

'Your private life, Charles. The prospect of crowning a libertine will not appeal to your more puritanical subjects.'

'Ah, the beautiful Barbara, wife to one of my most loyal subjects. Yes, I see your drift, James. You are right. Hostile elements in England could indeed use such a situation to their advantage.

'Have no fear, from now on I shall be discretion itself. A purer, more honest fellow you shall not find than I shall be.'

'You will discontinue your liaison with her then?'

'Discontinue what has only just begun? Not I! It is far too delightful to forgo so easily. God, she's the most tantalizing, fascinating woman I have ever bedded, James. You cannot ask me to give up what little pleasure I can derive from life, surely? But one thing I assure you, no one shall know of it. To all appearances she will be but a loyal lady of the court. Only you and I will know better.'

Charles laughed at James' disapproving look and put a friendly arm about his shoulder as they went to rejoin the others.

SEVEN

TOPAZ surveyed herself critically in the cracked looking-glass. The tan she had acquired in the weeks on the farm belied the weakness she still felt after the ague subsided. Today Franz would surely demand her to begin work in the tavern again—and all the horror that would entail.

The door opened and Klara stood on the threshold watching her. 'You'll pass,' she commented briefly. 'Come, there is work to be done.'

Topaz folded the shawl over her shoulders, naked in Klara's lowcut gown. 'You'll not need that now you are well,' Klara said, taking it sharply from her. 'Come.'

In the taproom Topaz could feel every man's eyes following her nakedness, and she was consumed with shame and misery. To her relief, however, no one made the familiar overtures to her that she had seen them make to Lisa. They laughed and joked and gave her handsome tips that caused Lisa to redden with anger.

'You have no right to take all that money,' she pouted sullenly in the kitchen. 'You should share it with us who have been here so much longer than you. I shall tell Klara so, and she'll make you share it, just you see.'

Topaz silently kept the coins in her pocket. She felt Lisa might have good grounds for envy, but every coin she earned would take her and her child so much nearer Charles, and with luck, without having to resort to means of earning it which she found repulsive. She had only to think of a hairy, revolting creature crushing her under his weight, and her hand kept tight hold on the money in her pocket.

That night she went to bed, happy and relieved that not one of the men had made an approach to her. She had heard Klara's door open and voices murmuring as she ushered a visitor out. Footsteps clattered on the staircase, and Franz's voice bade the visitor a hearty good night. Then he lowered his voice, but Topaz could hear his every word clearly.

'Is the wench abed, Klara, alone?'

'She is, but 'tis early days yet.'

Franz clicked his tongue in annoyance. 'It's that cold, pure look that frightens them off. You'll have to speak to her about it, Klara. Teach her how to coquette with them and lead them on, as Lisa and Hilde do.'

'She's better born than both Lisa and Hilde; she's no ordinary village wench, and I think the men sense it,' Klara replied thoughtfully. 'That they admire her is plain enough—Lisa tells me they tipped the girl handsomely. They're just a little apprehensive of her cool and distant shyness, it's not what they are accustomed to in a tavern pleasure-girl, but they'll overcome it.'

Franz snorted. 'Well, make it soon. She's been here over a week already, and not one client has she pleasured yet. Do not fail me, Klara.'

'Have I ever failed to train a girl yet?' Klara snapped. 'I've tamed wilder and shyer ones than her. Leave my job to me. And now, if you've no objection, Herr Franz, I am tired and must sleep.'

Topaz heard the door slam and Franz's footsteps retreat. How long, she wondered, could she keep the man at a distance and earn sufficient in tips to travel on? How long before Franz would press her into service?

She groped for the few coins under her pillow and counted

them. How many more would she need to be able to ride on the coach that plied regularly from here to Rotterdam? If only Charles knew of her plight. He was a man of means, she felt sure; he and James Butler were both business men, and he would be well able to pay her fare. If only he knew.

'How much money have we got between us, James?' Charles asked casually as they sat down at the card table to begin a game of hazard.

'Precious little. . . . I can advance you no more by way of stakes, if that is what you mean.'

'No, no. I need some cash to settle an outstanding debt, that is all,' Charles replied.

'Another card debt? Oh Charles! You promised you would run up no more!'

Charles smiled amiably. 'No more I have, my friend. This is to pay my laundress, Dorothy Chiffinch. I fear I have let the amount of my laundry bill run up somewhat, and my account with her is sadly in arrears.'

James sighed and leaned back in his chair, stretching out his velvet-clad legs, the easier to delve into his pocket. 'How far in arrears?' he asked.

Charles picked up his cards from the table, surveyed the hand a moment, then answered absently, 'About four and a half years now, by my reckoning.'

It was a few days later that one of the regular customers of the Nimble Rabbit finally plucked up courage to grab Topaz round the waist as she swept by, and gave her a resounding kiss on her cheek.

Topaz drew away in distaste, and saw Klara's observant eye on her, and her disapproving shake of the head. Later, in the kitchen, Klara drew her aside.

' 'Tis no use pulling such a face, mistress Topaz, when a gentleman shows his liking for you, or he'll not approach you again.'

'I do not want him to touch me again!' Topaz retorted.

Klara frowned. 'Now listen to me, my girl. You are no fool, and know full well what Herr Franz expects of you, do you not?' Topaz nodded miserably. Klara's face softened. 'And what is more, there are far more pickings to be gained by being amiable to the gentlemen than by scorning their advances.

'Come, look not so sad. Your pretty face and figure could gain you a mint of money and quickly, if you will but soften a little. These farmers have quite a few gold coins put by, and there's nothing that will make them part with their hard-earned money quicker than a handsome, willing wench.'

She put a finger under Topaz's chin and raised her face gently. 'No tears now. Be honest with yourself. You need the money, and what quicker way to earn it? Be off with you now, and no more of this false modesty—you cannot afford such extravagant notions.'

She turned Topaz towards the taproom door and gave her a gentle shove. Miserable and full of shame, Topaz went in. She had to admit, Klara was right. She would simply have to try to muffle all her sensibilities and revulsion and get on with the process of raising money.

'Mistress, more ale!' a hearty voice cried. Topaz straightened her shoulders and hastened to answer the summons. In the corner the big, blackbearded pirate of a man was teasing Lisa as she replenished his tankard. Topaz saw Lisa pout prettily and thrust her small, pointed breasts at him as she stood over him, then she bounced away back to the kitchen.

'Methinks the pert Lisa is of a mood to be taken tonight,' Topaz heard the big man say to his companion. 'No doubt she has heard that I fared well at the market today and has it in mind to help me dispose of the profits.' He chuckled heartily. 'We shall see. . . .'

His gaze lighted on Topaz and he beckoned her over. 'Bring us some roast pigeon, little one,' he said. 'Lisa dashed away too quickly to take our order.' Topaz saw his eyes following down the cleft in her bosom, and she wished she could cover herself. No, that was the wrong attitude; she must follow the example of the other girls.

'At once sir,' she replied in a low voice, and turned to go, but a strong hand held her wrist. The bearded man regarded her curiously.

'Tell me, child,' he said, 'have you your stallion for the evening picked out yet?'

Topaz coloured up furiously and wrenched her arm sharply but he did not let it go. 'Well, have you?'

'No sir.'

He smiled in satisfaction. 'Aha! Then I have a mind to be the first to test your paces, my little filly. Be so good as to tell Herr Franz I would speak with him,' he said, and let her go free.

Topaz ran into the kitchen, and delivered his order for the roast pigeon. 'What else did Herr Kestler say?' asked Franz who had been watching in the doorway.

'Nothing,' Topaz lied. May heaven forgive me, she said inwardly.

Lisa looked up sharply. 'Herr Kestler? He is always my customer, Herr Franz. Topaz has no business to be serving him,' she said.

'Hold your tongue, girl,' Franz snapped. 'The customers may take their own choice.' He turned to Topaz. 'I shall speak to Herr Kestler,' he said. 'Give me the pigeon to take him.'

A moment later he returned to the kitchen. 'Topaz, take Herr Kestler more ale. No Lisa, not you,' he added as Lisa made to go. 'He wishes to speak to Topaz.'

Lisa was red-faced with suppressed anger as Topaz went back to Herr Kestler's table. 'Will ten marks suit you, mistress?' he asked bluntly. Topaz was tongue-tied with shame, and wished she could sink through the floor. Suddenly Lisa's face appeared at her elbow, and she saw the girl's mouth drop open in amazement.

'You never gave me more than five!' she blurted angrily. Herr Kestler turned a look of irritable impatience upon her. 'You're my customer, Herr Kestler, and have been this twelve-month and more,' the girl cried miserably. 'Don't be taken in by her milk-and-water prettiness—she cannot satisfy you as I can! I know your little ways, and she does not!'

'Lower your voice, Lisa,' Herr Kestler snapped at her. 'Every man in the tavern is listening to you.'

'I won't be pushed out by this new chit!' Lisa's voice was rising to a hysterical crescendo. Topaz could bear no more of it, and ran towards the kitchen, tears of shame blinding her eyes. Franz stood in the doorway, blocking her escape.

'Enough of this nonsense!' he said roughly. 'Show Herr Kestler to your chamber at once.'

'I cannot,' Topaz moaned, the tears streaming down her face. 'I cannot do it!'

'You mean you will not!' Franz snarled. 'But I have waited long enough for you to begin work and will wait no longer. Upstairs!'

'No, No,' Topaz cried. 'Have pity, I beg you, do not make me do it!' Franz's only answer was a stinging blow across her cheek. His eyes glittered menacingly. Topaz's hand rose slowly and disbelievingly to her face. Behind Franz she could see Klara's face, her expression beseeching her to give in and avoid further trouble.

Dear heaven, Topaz cried inside herself, forgive me for what I am forced to do now. Is there no limit to the depths one can plough? In abject misery she stumbled slowly towards the staircase, and heard Herr Kestler jovially bid his companion good even. Then she heard his heavy footsteps mount the stairs behind her, and he hummed as he jingled the coins in his pocket.

As she reached the landing she was aware of a girl's sobbing protestations down below. That must be Lisa, disappointed and angry over her lover's fickleness. If only she and I could change places at this moment, Topaz thought.

Outside her chamber door a rough hand fell on her shoulder, and turned her about. Herr Kestler's air of casual indifference as he climbed the stairs had suddenly disappeared, and there was a gleam in his eyes that made Topaz suddenly recollect Detlev in the barn during the thunderstorm.

She felt his coarsened hand roughly pull down the front of her bodice and cup tightly under her breast, and lowered his face to hers. Topaz shut her eyes tight and felt sick with loathing. She felt his coarse curly beard on her cheek, and his breath stank of ale and schnapps as he pressed his thick lips on her own. Topaz's stomach retched, and she broke away and leaned her head against the wall, certain she was about to vomit.

'Come now, girl, do not waste my time,' he muttered sharply, and pulled her to him, throwing open the door to her chamber with his free hand. At that same second a whirling cloud of yellow satin skirts and frills hurtled towards them from the direction of the stairs. In his surprise Herr Kestler let go of Topaz, and Lisa sprang between them.

'Let him go, he's my client, he's always been my client!' Lisa screamed, her face contorted with fury. 'How dare you steal him from me, you cheap, tawdry slut!'

Topaz threw up her hands to protect her face from Lisa's flailing arms and fingernails. More footsteps thundered up the stairs, and Franz and Klara appeared suddenly behind Lisa. Klara leapt quickly between the two girls, and Lisa turned her vengeful spite then on Herr Kestler. Before he had time to act, she raised her hand and clawed him viciously across his face.

Franz grabbed her and pinioned her arms to her sides, then Klara gave her an echoing crack across her cheek. Instantly the girl's violence melted, and she whimpered like a whipped cur. Franz motioned to Klara to take her away. Herr Kestler dabbed at the blood that was beginning to seep through his beard, and Franz was at once all solicitude for his generous customer.

'I beg your pardon for the girl's behaviour, Herr Kestler,' he said humbly. 'I shall see to it personally that she is soundly whipped for her presumption. In the meantime Topaz will see to it that your face is bathed and your wants attended to, will you not, Topaz?'

He faced her with a meaningful look in his eye. Topaz was utterly bewildered by the events of the last few moments, and before she could reply, Herr Kestler was speaking.

' 'Tis nothing, 'tis only a scratch,' he laughed ruefully. 'God, but that Lisa has fire in her!'

'If it please you now to go into Topaz's chamber, I shall send up ale and whatever you require,' Franz went on persuasively.

'Do not trouble yourself, landlord; there's nothing like surprise attack to cause desire to die instantly. Another time, mayhap.' Herr Kestler turned to Topaz, and laughed softly as he saw her dismayed face. 'No offence, mistress. Your charms are many and obvious, if I may say so, but methinks Lisa was perhaps right and you are too gentle a filly for my hot blood.'

Topaz blushed furiously. He was referring to the ease with which she had become queasy at his eager touch. He bowed slightly, bid her good even, and moved away towards the stairs. Franz cast her a furious look, then followed Herr Kestler down, no doubt to continue his persuasive offers.

Topaz leaned against the wall and uttered a silent prayer of thanks for her deliverance. Miserably she prepared for bed, for it was late and the tavern was emptying, and it was unlikely Franz would send for her to come down again.

She lay on her bed and stared hopelessly at the rafters. Tonight she had been spared, but tomorrow inevitably she would have to lie and face those rafters with some other unwelcome client atop her.

Just in time she reached over for the pot before the vomit spurted from her mouth.

Charles lay on his side on the silken sheets, his hand supporting his tousled dark head, and watched the slender, shapely figure beside him move and stretch lazily like a cat. He ran his hand slowly down the smooth, silken skin and smiled appreciatively.

Violet-blue eyes flickered open slowly, and smiled lazily up at him. 'My liege?' a soft voice murmured.

Charles groaned. 'God, Barbara, you drive a man mad with desire! 'Tis but a half-hour since I took you last, and I could devour you yet again this instant.'

Barbara smiled. 'Then why hesitate, my lord? I am your loyal subject, whose only aim is to serve and please you.' She closed her eyes again and purred under his probing touch.

Charles' hand cupped tightly round a swelling white breast while the other entwined itself in her deep red hair.

'Take me, take me,' she murmured. 'I can never have you enough.'

Charles was content. What a fool James was, to expect him to give up a woman like this, a woman with the body of an angel and the same unbridled passion and delight in lovemaking as himself.

Life was sheer bliss at times like this. He delayed the moment of supreme pleasure as long as he could, but Barbara grew savage with impatience. Finally she enmeshed her fingers in his flowing locks and strained him close to her, moaning in sheer animal pleasure. Charles was ecstatic.

To hell with them all, Hyde and Butler and the others whose duty it was to guide and advise him! This woman he must keep!

EIGHT

NEXT day Lisa was soundly whipped for her behaviour, and returned to the kitchen, glowering menacingly at Topaz.

'I'll pay you out for this, my girl, just you see if I don't!' she hissed, brittle lights of hatred flashing in her green eyes.

Klara swept into the kitchen at that moment and bid Lisa to get on with her work. She watched thoughtfully as Topaz began washing dishes, but did not speak to her. Nor did Herr Franz when he came in soon afterwards to draw up a list of provisions.

Topaz found herself left much to her own thoughts that day. No one amongst the staff of the Nimble Rabbit went out of their way to speak to her, but she caught the girls eyeing her from time to time with a curious look.

The midday customers came and went, and Topaz could sense the air of constraint amongst them too. Not only did the men avert their eyes and fail to flirt and tease as usual, but it seemed that they preferred to call any of the other girls to serve them ale rather than Topaz. She began to wonder if Herr Franz had arranged this so that she would earn no more tips after her miserable failure last night with Herr Kestler.

One customer seemed glad of her services that evening, however. She caught sight of Hilde, a worried frown creasing her pretty face, trying hard to understand what a tall, fair, handsome youth was saying to her. He was a stranger to the tavern, and was waving his arms as he spoke. Out of curiosity Topaz drew closer to the young man. He was far better dressed than the local farmers, though his fine wool suit was creased and besmirched with mud and the expensive lace hung limply.

'Etwas zu essen,' he was saying. His German was halting and badly pronounced, but Topaz recognized with a start of excitement that he had the same English accent as Charles.

Hilde was still frowning and shaking her head in perplexity.

'Perhaps I can help you, sir,' Topaz cut in politely. The young man's face registered relief and surprise. Hilde turned away quickly, glad to be free of the problem.

'Oh thank heaven!' the young man smiled broadly at her. 'Be so good as to bring me and my companion some ale and whatever food you may have, for we are famished.'

'Glady, sir,' Topaz replied, and was aware of his surprise that she spoke his tongue. She hastened to the kitchen before he could question her, but she still felt his eyes following her.

On her return to the table she felt two pairs of eyes boring into her. The young man and his older companion watched her closely as she poured out the ale. Evidently they considered it ill-mannered to pry, to ask how she had learnt English. Perhaps they guessed the truth; that she was a person of culture who had fallen on hard times. But whatever the reason, they kept silent.

Later in the evening Topaz felt the young man's eyes still on her. He was standing by the door while his companion settled the reckoning with Herr Franz. There was admiration in his eyes, and his friend evidently noticed it for he nudged the Englishman in the ribs and joked, 'Come now Jason, there is no more time for eyeing the girls. We must be on the road again instantly.'

Jason nodded and turned, and the two men disappeared into the night.

Topaz, no longer needed in the taproom, busied herself in the kitchen. Lisa flashed her a malicious look of triumph whenever she passed, busily scurrying back and forth to the customers. She was obviously content that now she and Hilde were in demand again, and Topaz relegated to the dishes. Topaz was relieved to be left in peace.

But in a moment Klara came in, surveyed the pitchers on the floor, and then told Topaz to go quickly and fetch water from the tap in the yard to refill them.

Topaz took up a heavy pail and went out into the cold night air, glad to escape the heat of the kitchen for a few moments. Her eyes grew accustomed to the dark as she crossed the cobbles, and she saw a man taking two horses from the ostler under the torchlight near the inn door.

She recognized the older Englishman. Where then was the younger one, the one he called Jason, she wondered as she pumped water into the pail. She leapt in alarm as a strong arm snaked round her waist from behind her, and a low, resonant voice spoke in her ear.

'Do you come out to see us off, my pretty?' he said. He was smiling down at her, a pleasant, open smile. 'That was very civil of you—in fact, I think perchance I could gladly stay a little longer with a pleasant little maid like you.'

Topaz gathered her wits and answered with the pert, flighty manner that was expected of her. 'Faith, sir, you could hardly expect to keep your companion standing there holding your horse for the next half-hour while you amuse yourself!' she said lightly, and twisting out of his arm, she sped back to the kitchen door, as fast as she could with the heavy pail.

Behind her she could hear Jason's chuckle in the night, and it was some time later that she realized maybe she had been remiss in not asking the fair young Englishman whether he had ever heard of Charles Barlow.

Several days passed thus, and Topaz began to notice that even Franz was watching her closely and unsmilingly, and wondered why he made no comment.

It was Lisa who solved the riddle. She was in demand even more than usual that day, and when at last the afternoon brought its respite from the rush, she stood in the kitchen, one hand rested on the table and the other on her hip and she regarded Topaz with a gleam of satisfied triumph in her eye.

'So you see, mistress, they prefer me to you now,' she said with a wicked smile. Topaz continued scrubbing the deal table without answering. Lisa slid her hand into her pocket and withdrew a gold piece, which she flicked over in the palm of her hand. 'It serves you right for trying to steal Herr Kestler from me,' she said. 'There's not a man amongst 'em who will touch your fine body now, and precious few who want you near them at all. I saw to that,' she finished with a smile of cunning glee, and turned to go.

Klara was standing in the doorway. 'What means this talk, Lisa? What have you said to the customers?' she demanded.

Lisa's smile faded on the instant. She looked down sullenly at the floor. 'Come on, out with it girl,' Klara snapped, stepping forward and taking her by the shoulders.

'Stop, stop, I'll tell you!' Lisa cried when Klara began to shake her vigorously. Klara let her go, and she glared defiantly at Topaz. ' 'Twas her own doing! She lured Herr Kestler into her trap with her creeping, sly manner, and he's not the man to be taken in by any milksop. She must have given him a potion in his ale. She's a witch, I know she is! I told Hilde so, and some of the customers too!'

'You—did—what?' Klara's voice was incredulous. Topaz's breath was taken away by Lisa's astounding accusation, so that she was unable to deny the charge. Klara answered for her. Lisa shrieked and ran, clutching the throbbing ear that Klara had just severely boxed for her.

'What in the name of heaven is wrong with that girl now?' Franz strode into the kitchen from the yard. Klara explained, and Franz glowered at Topaz. 'Yes,' he muttered, 'she spoke to me of the matter. She said she had proof that the wench was a witch.'

Topaz was dumbstruck, but not so Klara. 'What proof? The girl is mad with jealousy, that is all. Did you believe her lies?'

Franz did not answer but busied himself with chopping meat. 'What proof?' Klara insisted, staying his arm. 'What did she say?'

Franz looked furtively at Topaz. 'She said she had three teats,' he muttered, his face red with confusion. 'She said that was clear proof she was a witch,' he blurted on, 'she had seen for herself, and knew that if anyone crossed Topaz, she could readily poison their ale or put a spell on them so that their crops would fail or their cows would not yield.'

Klara looked at him in amazement, then threw back her red hair and laughed scornfully. 'And you believed her!' she mocked.

'I knew not whether to believe her or not,' he retorted. 'but one thing I know. Since she came here nothing has gone well for us. Even the milk curdles.' He jerked his thumb at the porringer full of milk on the table. 'I do not wish to harbour one who may be in league with the devil,' Topaz heard him mutter as she turned and ran up to her chamber.

In the evening few customers came to the inn. Topaz found little to do in the kitchen, and Lisa and the other girls hung about talking in low voices in the taproom as if loth to share her company. Finally Klara sent her to bed.

Whispering voices outside her door awoke Topaz in the small hours of the night. Klara's voice cut in sharply, bidding the murmurers to get back to bed at once. Then quietly Topaz's door creaked open and Klara slipped in.

Her skirts rustled as she came closer. 'Topaz, are you sleeping?' she whispered.

Topaz sat up. Klara's face looked younger and less harsh in the moonlight that streamed in the tiny latticed window. She sat on the edge of the truckle bed and spoke gently.

'I do not wish to affright you, child, but you are in danger while you stay here,' she said. 'Lisa is bent on your destruction—I caught her just now plotting some mischief outside with Hilde. And in your condition it would not be safe to risk another fight with her.'

Klara saw the surprise in Topaz's face. 'I saw you were with child the day I gave you my gown to try. You turned your back when you changed, but my eye is accustomed to the curve of a woman with child, 'tis one of the risks of our trade that many who have worked here have had to endure,' she murmured.

Topaz realized then that this accounted for the care Klara had taken of her, and the way she had protected her from Franz's wrath. Gratitude welled up inside her. She reached for Klara's hand, but the older woman drew it away and stood up quickly.

"Full-bellied women are bad for trade in a pleasure house such as this,' she said sharply. 'And now even Franz fears your presence. 'Twould be best you left this place instantly.'

Her voice softened as Topaz rose and slowly began to dress, then hesitated. 'You may keep the clothes I gave you,' she said, 'but I fear they will grant you little enough warmth against the cold night.'

Topaz gathered together her meagre possessions and tied up the coins she had saved inside a strip of linen. 'Stay——' Klara added as Topaz bent to pick up her bundle, 'Franz's warm winter cloak hangs behind the kitchen door. Take it as you leave.'

Topaz began to murmur her thanks, but the woman brushed her aside. 'Be off with you now,' she whispered urgently as she opened the door, 'and take care no one hears you.'

As Topaz slipped quietly down the stairs she heard Klara's door close softly. In the kitchen she paused only to lift down the heavy woollen cloak from the hook before unlatching the door. Now I can even steal without a qualm of conscience, she thought. How much lower can I fall before finding my Charles again?

She crossed the cobbled inn yard, the chill night air biting through the cloak hastily thrown over her shoulders. Topaz drew it closer about her bare arms and wondered whether to await the coach close by, or to set off on the road towards the coast. If Lisa was bent on mischief, mayhap to put a distance between them both was the better idea.

She left the close-packed houses of the town behind her and began to walk in open country. Only occasional sounds like the hoot of an owl broke the silence, and Topaz began to feel nervous. She crossed herself anxiously and once again begged St. Teresa's protection.

A startled rabbit leapt from the hedgerow and ran across her feet to the far side of the road. Topaz bit back a scream and felt her child leap in alarm at the same moment. She patted her stomach reassuringly. 'Fear not, my child, we shall find your father ere long, and then we shall never need to fear anything again.'

Faintly in the distance she heard the clopping of hoofbeats. She was frightened and undecided whether to walk on, and perhaps be able to secure a lift with the passer-by, or to hide in case it was a robber. Few honest folk dared venture abroad at night, she knew, for fear of being waylaid and attacked by footpads or highwaymen. Discretion, she decided, was the best course, so she hid herself under a hedge and waited, hardly daring to breathe lest the rider should hear her in the stillness of the night.

As the sound came closer, Topaz heard also the rumbling sound of cart wheels, and gradually in the moonlight she made out the shape of a farm cart, coming from the same direction she had come, and with a solitary rider nodding on the box.

Slowly the cart rumbled past her. Silently Topaz stole out from her hiding place, placed her bundle on the tail board, then drew herself up on the cart and curled up behind the sacks. The driver did not stir. He was obviously sleeping and letting the horse find its own way home.

Topaz made herself as comfortable as she could, with her bundle for a pillow and empty sacks as covers, and despite the cart's swaying, jolting progress along the rutted lane, she finally slept.

Charles swept into James Butler's chamber at Breda. His face fell when he saw James' fat, fussy companion with the sheaf of papers in his hand.

'Ah Hyde, I did not expect to find you here,' Charles said, 'but now you are, let me tell you both how I found Minette.'

Both men turned, interest agleam in their eyes.

'Was Her Highness well?' Hyde enquired.

'Is she still as pretty?' said James. Charles laughed.

'Hyde is ever the politician and you the lady's man, James. Indeed, she is pretty, lovelier by far than I remembered her. Her hair is the most glorious light chestnut colour, and it goes stunningly with those deep blue eyes. Such a woman she has become! I'll wager half the nobles in France will hurl themselves at her feet ere long, the little beauty.'

He mused a moment. 'I' faith, she had changed so much I threw myself on the wrong girl by mistake!' he chuckled. 'That little wench was heartily taken aback when I kissed her roundly in mistake for my sister!'

Charles' smile faded fractionally, then a light frown crossed his forehead. 'Methinks Minette was mayhap a little too pale for my liking, and her lips showed all the redder for it. And there was just the hint of a curve in her spine that did not please me. . . . She could do with more exercise, I feel.'

Then his customary smile quickly replaced the shadow of a frown. 'But her eyes, James. You have only to look into her eyes and all else is forgotten but the desire to please her.'

Hyde cleared his throat. 'I am glad Your Majesty found Her Highness well and happy, and trust Her Majesty the Queen was also well. And now, if it please you, we have matters of importance to attend to.'

Charles sighed and looked expressively at James. Hyde's important matters were no doubt further unpaid bills he was anxious to call to Charles' attention, and Charles was not of a mood for such trivia tonight, when he was so happy.

And what was more, Barbara was awaiting him in his chamber, shining-eyed after his absence. He would cut this business as short as possible.

Topaz awoke with a violent jerk. The cart sloughed over on to one side into a runnel and its load slid rapidly to the edge. She could not save herself, but fell heavily over the tailboard and down a grassy bank into a ditch.

In the excrutiating pain that followed, threatening to snap her spine in half, Topaz was completely unaware of what happened to the driver of the cart. Nor at that moment did she care—her only awareness was of blistering, blinding pain searing round her waist and down her back. Its violence took her breath away so that she was unable to cry out. Vaguely she heard a bell clanging, then sank into merciful unconsciousness. . . .

A cool, musical sound forced Topaz to surface again through the layers of pain. Weakly she opened her eyes, but could not focus properly on the pale blue vision before her.

'Can you move, or shall I fetch help?' The sounds made

sense this time. A woman's voice hovered in the half-light of dawn, and gradually Topaz's eyes cleared and she saw a woman in a blue habit leaning over her. The pain ebbed slowly and Topaz drew a deep breath.

'Heaven be praised, I feared you were dead,' the gentle voice said. 'Let me help you rise, and we shall see whether you can walk.' She drew Topaz's arm around her neck and strained to lift her, but in vain. Topaz felt useless; she could no longer feel her legs, only a swollen numbness from her waist down.

'No matter,' the woman said. 'The convent is close by. I shall fetch help and be back instantly. Meanwhile, do you rest easy.'

The waves of pain began to return, growing fiercer and more devouring at every second. Topaz gasped and writhed. Hazily she felt herself being lifted and carried, but was aware only of the overwhelming pain that forced sobs from her throat despite herself. After what seemed centuries, she was grateful to feel warm, soft covers drawn over her, and she sank down through the layers of pain into oblivion.

Charles moaned in ecstasy. What infinite joy and pleasure Barbara granted him! She never failed him; however long their partings, they seemed able to come together again in mutually gratifying passion and without having to waste too much time on all the courtly preamble other women expected and needed. She was a jewel, indeed she was!

Beneath him Barbara's movements gathered momentum, and within seconds she too was arching back her head and exhaling a long, purring sigh of satisfaction.

Well, enough is as good as a feast, Charles decided. They had celebrated their reunion right royally tonight, and dawn was beginning to glimmer through the window already.

He rolled over and buried his head in the pillows. Within moments he was blissfully asleep.

Topaz's eyes flickered open. It was a tremendous effort to lift those heavy lids, but when her eyes became accustomed to the gloom she saw she was in a low truckle bed in a small, bare chamber. Mercifully the pain had fled, and now all she felt was weakness and utter weariness.

She struggled to sit up, but was too weak. Through the mist she made out the shape of a large crucifix on the whitewashed stone wall facing her. Slowly her memory returned. The fall from the cart—the agonizing pain—the woman in blue—a nun, was it?—and her soft, musical voice.

The handle of the door rasped and turned. A figure in blue holding a sputtering tallow candle glided in and came close to the bed.

'Ah, you're awake at last,' said the lilting voice Topaz remembered. A cool hand passed over her brow. 'Rest you now, my child, do not try to move,' she said. ' 'Twas a bad fall you must have had, and 'twill be a mercy if you do not lose your child. Are you in pain?'

Topaz rolled her head from side to side, but could not find the strength to speak, to ask where she was, and who the kindly nun. The woman seemed to read her thoughts.

'My name is Sister Maria,' she murmured. 'You are safe in the convent of Schlectergard, so you need have no fear. No one can pursue you here, and none would dare to defy Mother Louisa to try to drag you forth for punishment. Commit yourself into God's hands, my child. My sisters and I will do what we can for you and your child.'

She smiled and turned to the door. 'Sleep easy now, and we shall talk more in the morning. Good night and God bless you, child.'

In the halo of light from the candle surrounding her wimple she looked like a vision of Our Lady, thought Topaz. I am indeed in good hands, and can sleep in peace tonight, so long as my child is well.

She pressed her hands to her stomach. The bulge still rose, bulky and unmoving, under her palms. She had not lost her babe after all. Silently she prayed and thanked God for their safety, and begged once again to be allowed to find Charles. In time, when she was well enough, she would press onwards, but for the moment she could rest in this haven of peace.

NINE

LOW voices at the foot of the bed caused Topaz to awake. It was full daylight already and watery sunshine filtered in through the tiny barred window.

'How came she here?' the voice of an older woman was saying.

'I found her in the ditch when I went to see to Joachim's cart,' replied Sister Maria. 'He came back in the night, rather the worse for ale, and said the cart had overturned just as he approached the gate. She was lying there, and obviously in pain.'

'I see. And you say she is with child?'

'Yes, Reverend Mother, but she was like to lose it in the night. She bled heavily, but thank God the bleeding has stopped now.'

'A bastard child, is it?'

'I know not, Reverend Mother, but as you see, her hands are ringless.'

'And her clothes are those of a tavern wench,' the older woman retorted in disgust. Topaz opened her eyes and saw her holding Topaz's gown in outstretched fingers, eyeing its brazen immodesty. She looked up and caught Topaz's gaze.

'Aha! Awake, my child?' She advanced closer and surveyed her thoughtfully.

Topaz saw the lined, careworn face of a small woman in the same blue habit as Sister Maria, but she had an undoubted air of authority about her. Her eyes held a kindly light despite the severity in her voice.

'Running away, child, friendless and penniless?' she asked. 'Casting yourself on the mercy of strangers?'

Topaz strained to find her voice. 'I go to seek my husband,' she whispered. 'He will marry me, when he knows. And I am not quite penniless—there is a little money in my bundle—I will pay for my keep.' Pride forced her to speak. She could not bear that these holy women should take her for a promiscuous jade for any village lad to take.

The Mother Superior's face softened. 'There is no need for payment,' she said. 'You can help with the work in the kitchen until your time comes, and then you can decide when to move on. There is no need for you to make any decision just now. For the sake of your child, rest easy. Sister Maria will take care of you, and when you are better, she will direct you what work you are to do.'

Before Topaz could offer her thanks, the woman nodded to Sister Maria and swept out.

Within a few days Topaz was on her feet again, though still somewhat weak and confused. Sister Maria had taken away the gown Klara had given her, and brought a warmer one of sober brown worsted in its place. It seemed to Topaz that the weather was unusually cold for November, and she could barely refrain from shivering. Sister Maria conducted her to the kitchen, and as Topaz followed her along the cold, silent corridors of the convent, she was glad she was to work in the kitchen where at any rate there would be warmth from the fire.

Sister Maria explained that theirs was a contemplative order, and though they had not taken a vow of silence, nevertheless they did not speak except when necessary. Thus Topaz was prepared for the quietness in the kitchen, but nonetheless it seemed eerie to watch silently busy figures flitting to and fro on noiseless mule-clad feet.

How strange and tranquil it was, and how different from

the noisy, raucous chatter in the kitchen of the Nimble Rabbit! A joint turned slowly on a spit, watched over by a pale young nun. The crackling of the fat as it dripped into the fire, and the bubbling cauldron of water were the only sounds to be heard in the vast, stone-flagged room, until a pudgy, red-faced nun began pounding with a pestle and mortar.

It was surprising how smoothly the work progressed, thought Topaz as she sat at the trestle table scraping carrots. A smile, a nod, one forefinger raised conveyed all the messages necessary from one nun to another.

Suddenly a bell clanged and Topaz started. Immediately every nun rose and walked slowly, head downcast and hands clasped, towards the door. Of course, it was midday, and the Angelus. They would be going to the chapel. Topaz rose and followed them.

It was odd, yet refreshing, to be ignored, she reflected. No one made demands on her; how different from the Nimble Rabbit! In the chapel she gave thanks again for this unexpected peace and restfulness.

Day followed day in the same quiet, yet busy manner. Topaz still did not feel very strong, and one day to her surprise she awoke to find her legs were swollen and aching.

She would not mention it, she decided. All these holy women here laboured on silently and uncomplainingly and she could do likewise. She remembered in the Refectory one day a young nun had raised her habit to step over a bench and Topaz had caught a glimpse of an open, suppurating ulcer on her leg.

Topaz had told Sister Maria about it, for it was she who tended all sickness within the convent. She described the young nun to her.

'That will be young Sister Felice who works in the fields,' Sister Maria had nodded.

'Will you see to her?' Topaz had asked.

Sister Maria had thought a moment, then she shook her head. 'It is not for me to interfere,' she said gravely. 'My sisters believe that mortification of the flesh is good for the soul. It is possible Sister Felice is offering up her suffering to God for her soul's future salvation. If she decides treatment is necessary she will approach me when she is ready.'

So why should Topaz complain now of her swollen legs? It would seem a small matter in comparison with Sister Felice's ulcer. Like her holy sister, Topaz could offer up the pain to God. So with difficulty she walked about her work, trying as hard as she could not to limp.

But oh! the cold! Try as she might, Topaz could not refrain from shivering as she worked in the kitchen, close as she was to the roaring fire. The cold seemed to eat into her bones and cause her legs to cramp and ache all the more. None of the other kitchen workers appeared to notice the cold; on the contrary, they stopped from time to time to wipe the perspiration from their brows.

Day followed day in the same silent routine, and still Topaz felt weak and hazy. She knelt in the chapel one evening at Vespers, watching the face of the Mother Superior, and to her surprise she saw two faces, side by side. Topaz looked away quickly and caught Sister Maria's watchful eye upon her. Two Sister Marias were watching her! Topaz was terrified. It was some trick of the devil, even in this holy place! She closed her eyes tightly and prayed for St. Teresa's protection.

As she left the chapel, Sister Maria touched her on the elbow. 'How is it with you, child? I feared you did not look well this evening.'

' 'Tis nothing, 'twill pass,' said Topaz quickly, but still two faces of Sister Maria kept superimposing one on the other, then separating again. Topaz swayed and Sister Maria took her tightly by the arm, calling Sister Felice to come and help her.

Back in her own cell, Topaz was quietly stripped and put to bed. Heavens, the cold! It seemed to penetrate the blankets and gnaw deep into her flesh. Topaz shuddered violently and her legs cramped viciously. She cried out in pain, then to her alarm her body seemed to act of its own accord. Her back arched up, flexed and rigid, and her teeth clenched tight, cutting into her tongue.

Terror seized her. She was imprisoned inside this body which had a will of its own! Sister Felice was looking in horror at the foam gathering on her lips. 'Holy Mother of God!' she cried suddenly, seizing Sister Maria's arm in terror, 'She is possessed! See how she rages—for her sins the devil has possessed her!' She sank on her knees in abject fear, crossed herself quickly and prayed aloud in a high-pitched squeak.

Sister Maria grabbed her by the arm and pushed her out of the door. Topaz saw it all, but thought of nothing but her own terror-stricken helplessness. Finally she fell unconscious. . . .

Voices filtered to her through the mist. 'Swollen legs . . . child is not moving . . . then this fit,' she heard the unmistakable lilting voice of Sister Maria say. ' 'Twould be best to rid her of her burden now, or mayhap it will be too late.'

Too late. . . . Too late. . . . The words sounded again and again like a knell. Bells were ringing in Topaz's ears, a low, sombre clang, as at a requiem mass.

Sister Maria bent over her, pouring a vile-tasting liquid between her lips. 'Drink, my child, it is for the best,' she heard her say. It could be poison for all Topaz knew or cared at that moment. Some outside force other than her own will seemed to have taken possession of her, and if it was the devil's work, then death seemed the only solution.

Death? Oh no, not when she still had Charles and his child to think of! It was unthinkable, despite the pain. Forgive me,

St. Teresa, for the vile thought; help me, for God's sake, help me!

But heaven seemed to close its ears to her cry. The one clear, unmistakable fact that came through to Topaz in her delirium was the voice of Sister Maria, overflowing with pity and regret.

'It is sad, Reverend Mother, but I fear the fall occasioned more harm than we thought. It is clear she carries a dead child in her womb, and unless she is rid of it soon, it must needs poison and kill her.'

Dead child! Dear God, what have I done? Topaz could not see her own danger, only her dismal failure. By her actions she had killed Charles' child! She gave up the attempt to cling to reason and sanity and sank into an abyss of despair. What matter now whether she lived or died?

She drank the evil potion gratefully.

Hell had its way with Topaz. Demons tore her limb from limb and devoured her piecemeal. The agony was as nothing to her, if it helped to atone for her sins. She succumbed to it all in utter submission. Wave after wave of anguish crashed upon her weakened body, then receded a moment before crashing upon her shattered frame again. Topaz offered no resistance, and centuries later it was with utter disbelief that she finally opened her eyes.

Sister Maria stood framed in the patch of light from the little window. In her blood-stained hands she held a tiny figure.

'Am I still alive?' Topaz whispered, unable to believe it.

Sister Maria smiled. 'By the help of God, my child, you live but I fear your child does not.' She laid the little body aside on a chest and came to Topaz's side. 'You must rest, for I fear it was a long, hard struggle and you lost much blood. But with care, you will grow strong again.'

Topaz struggled to sit up, but Sister Maria's firm hand

restrained her. 'You have been long abed, my child, and very ill. Christmas has come and gone while you struggled to live.'

Christmas? Then those were the bells Topaz had heard in her delirium! Sister Maria evidently saw the incredulity in her face, for she added softly, 'Indeed, 'tis now the year of Our Lord sixteen-hundred and sixty, and 'tis sincerely to be hoped this year holds more happiness for you than the last.'

She turned quietly and left the room, her habit swishing gently as she moved. Topaz lay and tried to gather her confused thoughts together. So it would seem the fires of hell had been but the pains of labour—and to what end? She looked across to where her child lay, inert, on the chest. A bowl of water stood beside it.

Sister Maria had not said whether it was a boy or a girl. And what was to become of the child's body? Would it be buried in some unconsecrated spot, an unbaptized bastard? Topaz shrank from the cruel thought. Baptized at least it *must* be. But how was she to ensure that a priest would baptize the little creature, to save it from the eternal frustration of limbo, neither heaven nor hell? There was only one way to be sure—to baptize the little dead thing herself. Sister Maria would no doubt return to collect it at any moment—she must see to it now!

Topaz lifted the bedcovers feebly and dragged her legs out over the side of the low bed. It was a tremendous effort to sit upright, and then her strength seemed to ebb. To crawl would be easier than to walk across the room. She lowered herself to the floor, and with enormous effort she crawled, inch by inch, across the intervening space.

By the chest she stopped, gasping, and hauled herself up. As her face drew level with the top, she stopped and gazed at the infant. It was a tiny boy, and Topaz's breath locked in her throat as she looked at his miniature face. Black hair surrounded a grave little face. He was a replica of Charles.

She dipped her fingers in the bowl of water and splashed the infant's face. 'I baptize thee, Karl, in the name of the Father, and of the Son, and of the Holy Ghost,' she whispered. Sobs burst free from her throat as her strength gave out and she slipped down on the cold stone floor. Oh Charles, forgive me! I have done what I can for our son! she sobbed.

Sister Maria was hurt and reproachful as she put Topaz back into bed, but Topaz did not hear her. All she was aware of was the fact that she had failed her beloved Charles.

'God!' exclaimed Charles, 'but it's cold here in Flanders. I'll warrant there's not a creature on earth has suffered more from the cold than we have this past month!' He crouched low over the fire, stretching out his chilled fingers to the low flame.

' 'Tis not every man has to keep body and soul together on the pittance we do,' replied James. 'But the way matters are moving in England now, it may not be for long.'

Hyde clicked his tongue impatiently. 'Just because Monk has at last taken the step of invading England there is no reason yet to suppose he is for restoring the monarchy. And yet you may be right; I can feel in my bones there is change astir.'

Charles chuckled. 'Any change will be most welcome. Greater poverty than ours there cannot be, nor a more biting cold in all the world.'

He rose and stamped fiercely up and down the chamber, flinging his arms energetically across his chest in an effort to thaw his freezing limbs.

James gazed into the dying embers. 'Aye, our debts have never been greater,' he murmured, 'but there must be some poor devils worse off than ourselves.'

'You think so?' Charles stopped in surprise. 'I would have thought it impossible that anyone could have suffered more than we have this winter. If there is anyone, it is not anyone I know, that's for sure.'

The only place in Brussels he could be sure of warmth, he reflected, was in bed with a warm and willing woman. Thank heaven for warm-hearted women!

Topaz's child was buried, and with his interment she endeavoured to bury all her thoughts and regrets of the past. Her mind seemed incapable of functioning or her emotions of feeling any more. It was as though labour and the death of the child had used up the last ounce of her feelings. Now she felt only numbness and a feeling of no longer having any aim in life.

Sister Maria nursed her devotedly and Topaz felt sorry for her. It must be like nursing a statue, devoid of feeling, and without any will to live. Day after day she saw Sister Maria gaze anxiously into her face for a sign of improvement, but Topaz just lay there dispassionately.

Then one day she caught sight of her own face reflected in the highly polished glass of the jug beside her bed. Dear heaven! That was never her face! She peered closer. Sunken eyes lay open, blank and dull in a pasty, shadowed countenance. Lank, dun-coloured hair dropped on her shoulders. Was this the face Franz had counted on to attract custom to his inn? A man would have to be in dire straits indeed to be attracted to that same face now!

Topaz felt ashamed of herself. Thank heaven Charles could not see her wallowing thus in self-pity! She must try and pull herself together, for his sake. He would be sorry about the babe, of course, but she was young yet and could be healthy again if she put her mind to it. There could be many more babes for her and Charles.

If she could find him. That was her goal, to find Charles. But how? And where? It was spring again now—almost a year had elapsed since he left. He could be anywhere in Europe!

Topaz lay back despondently on the pillows. It was useless. Maria bustled in.

The door opened and Reverend Mother glided in. She seated herself near the bed and looked thoughtfully at Topaz.

'How fare you now, my child?' she asked gently. Topaz answered that she felt better, grateful that the Reverend Mother was so concerned for her welfare, despite the fact that she obviously took her for a harlot.

'The weather is brightening and spring is coming,' said the older woman. 'Perhaps it is time you rose from your bed and made some attempt to enter the world again. One cannot hide from life for ever.'

She paused and cocked her head on one side to watch Topaz's reaction. Topaz blushed.

'I feel perhaps I should explain to you, Reverend Mother, how I came to be on the road alone, and with child, when Sister Maria found me. I am no cheap tavern wench, as you may be forgiven for believing, but fate drove me to the state in which you found me.'

Reverend Mother laid her hand on Topaz's arm. 'There is no need to explain if you do not wish to, my child. I know from your behaviour here, your patience in all your trials and your devout piety, that you are not what I mistook you for. I pray heaven, and you too, Topaz, will forgive my suspicious thoughts.'

Topaz, however, felt that she owed the kindly sisters an explanation after all their zealous care of her. When she had finished, the older woman's eyes were full of pity and concern.

'I shall pray for you, as we all shall,' she said softly. 'As soon as you feel able to face the world outside again, I would advise you to travel on in your search.'

Reverend Mother left an aura of peace and goodwill in the little cell behind her. Topaz lay luxuriating in the tranquil atmosphere. Maria bustled in.

'Come now, enough of this lying abed,' she said briskly. 'You cannot spend all your days in idleness, another pair of hands is needed in the kitchen, for we are to have company tonight.' She held out Topaz's gown.

Topaz looked up, idly curious. 'Company?' she asked.

Sister Maria nodded. 'A lady is to stay the night on her way to Rotterdam.' And as Topaz drew on her gown she added, 'A real lady, a titled English lady.'

Topaz's interest was aroused at once. English? Perhaps—it was just possible—the lady might have heard of Charles Barlow!

TEN

TOPAZ felt the first tingling of anticipation stirring within her as she brushed her long hair vigorously and pinched her sallow cheeks in an effort to bring back some colour to them.

Her legs stumbled a little as she walked down the empty corridor. Weeks of lying abed had made them weak, but the prospect of company, and English company at that, gave her added energy and the will to walk.

The nuns at work in the steamy kitchen gave her kindly smiles to welcome her back, but did not speak. It was as she was making her way up to the Refectory for the evening meal that she first caught sight of the visitor about to enter the Mother Superior's study. The small plump lady, heavily beringed and wrapped in a warm riding cloak, turned a beaming smile upon her, then followed the Reverend Mother through the oaken door.

After supper Topaz loitered in the corridor in the hope of seeing her again. She was lucky. As Reverend Mother emerged with the lady, she saw Topaz and called her over. 'I am glad to see you are up and about, my child,' she said, then turned to the visitor. 'This, my lady, is Topaz, a little maid who is also staying with us at the moment. As she also speaks your tongue, mayhap she will help you pass the evening hours pleasantly.'

She laid a hand gently on Topaz's shoulder. The lady smiled again and nodded her acknowledgement. Reverend Mother then addressed Topaz. 'Lady Davenham stays but this one night with us, Topaz, on her way to Rotterdam. Would you like to show her to her room and then make her comfortable? Mayhap the library is free and you may talk there.'

For the first time in months Topaz felt pleased. The prospect of talking to this woman with such a warm, agreeable appearance was indeed attractive, and it was just remotely possible if English exiles clung together in a group, that she knew Charles.

She led Lady Davenham to her cell and helped her remove her cloak and hat. Having satisfied herself that she had dined at an inn not long before, she then took her to the library where a roaring fire blazed in the hearth.

'Pray you, be seated,' said Topaz, indicating a chair by the fire. The lady sat, arranging her silk gown about her as she did so. Her rings caught and flashed back the firelight. Topaz had never seen a more magnificent creature, and thought how dismal she herself must look, with her pallid face and drab worsted gown.

'Come child, sit here beside me.' Lady Davenham indicated a joint stool beside her chair. Topaz was glad it was near the fire, for the cold of the winter still persisted although it was March already.

'How are you named, child?' the lady enquired softly.

'Topaz Birke, if it please you, my lady.'

'Indeed it pleases me—a mighty pretty name Topaz. But be not so formal. Call me Lady Arabella. How came you to this place, Topaz? Are you a novice?'

'No, ma'am.'

'Forgive me, I did not mean to pry. But you do not appear to be a servant and I was curious.'

Topaz did not answer. She did not mean silently to rebuke Lady Arabella's curiosity, but it was difficult to explain to a stranger the reason for her presence in the convent without sounding as though she was spinning some pitiful tale, to gain sympathy.

Her perplexity must have shown on her face, for suddenly Lady Arabella threw back her head and laughed. It was a gentle laugh, like the tinkling of a bell.

'My daughter—Sophie—often reproaches me for poking my nose into where I have no business to pry. She wears just the same frown as you do now when I quiz her. Really, I think the young today hate to share their thoughts with their elders. They think we have never undergone the same trials ourselves in the past.'

She talked rapidly and easily, as though to cover Topaz's discomposure, Topaz thought. She spoke of her children, Sophie and her son, whom she was to rejoin in Rotterdam. She cocked her head on one side and looked thoughtfully at Topaz.

'Sophie is not unlike you in appearance—fairhaired and small-featured, but she is several years older than you and some few inches taller.' She sighed a long-drawn-out sigh. 'Twenty-five she was last October, and nary a husband in sight yet. Too clever, that's her problem. Frightens all the men away who seek only a pretty face and amiable companionship.'

Topaz warmed to this graceful, kindhearted creature, and thought how graceless she was to be so taciturn in her company. As the evening wore on, Topaz talked more freely to her, and divulged that she had been in retreat in the convent and was now recuperating from recent illness.

Lady Arabella smiled knowingly. 'I knew you were no servant,' she said. 'You have a graceful hearing and the courteous manners that no servant ever acquired, and your command of our language is excellent.' She leaned forward and tapped Topaz on the knee. 'I think, in these dark days of intrigue, you are really some member of a European royal family parading under an incognito!' She winked broadly.

Topaz laughed aloud. Lady Arabella was really delightfully

easy to befriend, with her joyful, mischievous air of a child. Then Lady Arabella began to speak of her friends in Rotterdam and of their long exile from home. Thus it came about that Topaz was at length able to utter the question she was burning to ask.

'Is there perchance among your circle a Mr. Barlow?' she asked diffidently enough, but her heart was leaping as she said his name. 'A Mr. Charles Barlow, a merchant? I met him once, a year or so ago in Germany,' she added by way of explanation. She felt ashamed at the half-truth. To make her and Charles' meeting and loving sound like a casual encounter was treachery. She crouched on her stool, her hands on her cheeks to hide the blush that rose unbidden.

Lady Arabella was an eternity in replying. She frowned as she racked her memory, and finally shook her head dubiously. 'Barlow? I cannot recall the name. . . . Though that signifies little, for I have a monstrous bad memory for names.' The frown suddenly changed to a smile. 'Sophie will know. I'll ask her tomorrow.'

Topaz could ask no more questions, for Lady Arabella rose to her feet and yawned politely behind her hand. ' 'Tis past the time I usually go to my bed. If you will forgive me, Topaz. . . .'

Topaz went to open the door for her. In the doorway Lady Arabella paused and looked at her thoughtfully. 'Have you any plans for when you leave here, child?'

Topaz shook her head slowly.

'I was just wondering . . .' Lady Arabella mused. 'Sophie is seeking a companion. And as events in England are moving so fast now and the chances are that we may return to London before long, she will need a companion then for all the social life.'

'Return to London?' Topaz could not help repeating in surprise.

'Yes. Why, have you not heard General Monk is in charge of London, Parliament is to be dissolved after all these years, and, God willing, King Charles may soon be restored? My dear child, all Europe is buzzing with the news. English people are hastening back to Rotterdam to be ready to sail for home once the General comes out for monarchy.'

She gazed at Topaz in surprise, then recollected. 'But I forget, you have been in retreat, locked away from the world. How could you know?'

She squeezed Topaz's arm gently. 'But if you have no other plans, think of my suggestion. If you and Sophie find each other agreeable, well and good. If you do not, then at least the trip to Rotterdam will do you good. You look as if some fresh air would benefit you, child.

'I leave soon after daybreak. If you wish to come with me, be packed and ready. I shall not be offended if you consider me rash and impulsive and decline to come. But I know when I like people, and I felt an instant rapport with you, Topaz.'

Her bell-like laugh tinkled merrily again. 'Dismiss me as a foolish old woman if you will, my dear, but I must away to my bed now.' And in a mist of delicate musk-like perfume she turned and was gone.

Topaz had no hesitation in deciding what to do. If English people were preparing to return to their own country, then there was no time to be lost in tracing Charles. She *must* go with Lady Arabella tomorrow.

As she hurried back to her cell to gather her belongings Topaz's legs no longer felt weak. It was surprising how strengthening it was to have a purpose in life once again.

At first light Topaz was ready. Bundle in hand and her cloak over her arm, she sought out Sister Maria to bid her farewell and found her already at prayer in the chapel. Seeing Topaz, she crossed herself, rose and came out.

'So you have decided to go with Lady Davenham,' she said. 'Reverend Mother told me this morning of my lady's proposal. I hope all goes well for you now, child. You are wise to move on, not to stay here and mope.'

Topaz tried to utter her thanks for Sister Maria's loving care of her, but the older woman cut her short. 'Say no more. It is recompense enough that you are alive and well. God in His mercy heard our prayers for you, Topaz, and I pray He will take good care of you now. Now go make your farewells to Reverend Mother.'

She turned Topaz about and pushed her gently. 'God bless you, child,' Topaz heard the soft musical voice say as she walked away. And you, too, Sister, Topaz murmured.

Lady Arabella was ready cloaked and gloved in the vestibule, and Reverend Mother was with her. Her face lit up when she saw Topaz.

'You are coming after all?'

'If you will be so good as to take me, my lady.'

'I shall be delighted!' Lady Arabella turned to the Mother Superior. 'Then we must away, for the coach stands waiting. Thank you for your kindness and hospitality, Reverend Mother.'

Reverend Mother smiled. 'It is we who should thank you, for our chapel will gain handsomely from your generous donation, my lady.'

Lady Arabella smiled happily, 'And you need have no fear for Mistress Topaz, for I shall guard her well,' she said.

'I could commit her into no better hands, of that I am sure,' Reverend Mother replied as they walked out of the convent entrance.

Within moments Topaz was speeding away from the convent in the dusky light of dawn, to a new life. Eager hope warmed her bones against the chillness of the spring morning.

Charles and Edward Hyde were poring over a list of accounts when James entered the study and flung himself in a chair.

'Any news from England this bright morning, James? Has Monk declared yet?' Charles asked him cheerfully enough, but there was a note of anxiousness in his voice.

James shook his head. 'Sir John Grenville is making attempt to see him privately, but the General is too cautious to welcome the King's representative openly. So far he has declined to meet him. We must have patience yet.'

Charles' sunny smile returned. 'I am content enough as matters are, and so is Hyde, I warrant. Since my prospects have become so much rosier, those who erstwhile scorned me, a penniless exile without land or title, are suddenly very anxious to dine me and foot my bills, are they not, Hyde?' He jingled the gold coins in his pocket merrily. 'I must have had a hundred guineas poured into my pockets in the last day or two alone!'

'One hundred and four, to be precise,' said Hyde looking at his figures.

'To blazes with the four! I can afford to squander that now! God, but it's wonderful to feel money in one's pockets again after all those years of penury!'

'The tide of public opinion is certainly in your favour now,' James commented. 'I hear English exiles all over Europe are flocking back to the coast to be ready for the announcement. There is an air of happy excitement I cannot remember seeing since Her Majesty your mother gave birth to you.'

Charles smiled happily. 'And when I am restored to the throne, that is the way I intend to keep it. Happiness shall be the order of the day in our country.'

Hyde grunted and gathered up his papers.

By dusk that evening the long, jolting coach journey was

over and Topaz felt the cobblestones of Rotterdam under the wheels. The coach drew up in the yard of a small white house, beautifully clean and brightly lit.

'Home at last,' sighed Lady Arabella in relief as the servants hastened out to lower the step and unload the luggage. She leaned her weight heavily on the arm of the manservant who helped her down the steps, and Topaz followed her up the flight of stone stairs to the door.

A tall, fairhaired young woman stood at the top, her dull gold gown gleaming softly in the light of the torch held by another servant. She held out her arms to Lady Arabella, who fell upon her, embracing her warmly and cooing with delight.

'My dear, you look ravishing!' she cried. 'Only a week I've been away from you, and I swear you've grown far lovelier than ever before!'

'Mother, really!' the girl remonstrated quietly, then she looked curiously at Topaz.

'Oh forgive me, my dear. This is Mistress Birke, a friend I met at the convent. Her name is Topaz. Is that not a beautiful name? Topaz, this is my daughter I spoke of, Sophie. I hope you two will be good friends.'

Topaz felt the other girl's eyes appraising her with a cool, calculating look. She knew she was taking in the mean, drab gown and cloak and the hair which was evidently not dressed by a lady's maid. No doubt she was wondering why her generous, impulsive mother had picked up such a pauper, but she was too well-mannered to ignore Topaz.

'Please don't stand out here in the cold,' Sophie said taking her mother's arm. 'There is a warm fire in the library and a good meal almost ready. Let me take your cloak.'

She helped her mother lay aside her cloak, beckoning to a servant to see to Topaz, then led the way into the library. A glowing log fire cast long shadows on the oak-panelled walls, lined with bookshelves. Sophie called for more light, and a servant took a taper to the wax candles in their sockets on the walls.

This room, with its panelled walls, put Topaz in mind of the parlour at Torwald, but this room was far more gracious; rugs were scattered on the floors and silver vases held a profusion of spring flowers. Kaspar hated flowers in the house, even in the oratory. It was odd, Topaz thought, but Kaspar and Torwald had hardly ever come into her thoughts since the day she left there.

Hannah, however, frequently came into her mind. Dear, kind Hannah who had been the only mother she had ever known, and who would no doubt still be fretting as to what had become of her. Hannah and Lady Arabella had quite a lot in common, she reflected, with their plump, warm motherliness.

She looked across at Lady Arabella who was leaning forward in her chair as she talked eagerly to Sophie about the incidents of the past week.

'Aunt Matilda was well and sends you her love and hopes we shall all be together again soon in London,' she was saying, and Sophie on the other side of the hearth was listening intently and nodding.

Suddenly there was a sound of a heavy door slamming, boots clattering in the vestibule, and a man's voice calling a servant. Sophie smiled.

'Ah, I think my errant brother has returned at last,' she said. 'Now we can all eat together. I shall go and see if supper is ready.'

She swept smoothly out of the room. Lady Arabella sighed and stretched. 'Oh, it's so nice to be home again, in the bosom of one's family,' she murmured. 'Visiting one's relations is fun, but travelling is so tiring.'

In moments Sophie was back. 'Come,' she said. 'Supper is ready, so let us eat before the soup goes cold.'

As they entered the dining-room Topaz could see a round table laid with a white damask cloth and gleaming cutlery. Lady Arabella shrieked with pleasure and hastened forward, her arms outstretched.

Topaz stood by the door. A young man, his back towards her, was bending over a side table, reading a paper. Lady Arabella threw her arms about his neck and hugged him close.

The young man finally disengaged himself and smiled down fondly at her. Topaz saw his profile with a start of surprise. 'That's a fine welcome, Mother,' he said, and Topaz recognized the deep, velvety tone of his voice.

'My dear,' said Lady Arabella, 'I want you to meet a friend of mine, Topaz Birke. Topaz, this is my son, Jason.'

Lady Arabella was smiling proudly but Topaz did not see her. She was staring in disbelief at the young man. It was the young Englishman she had once served at the Nimble Rabbit, the one who could not speak German. She had helped him—he must remember her!

Please, please, let him have forgotten the sleazy little inn on the Dutch border, and the half-naked pleasure-girls who served there.

Oh heaven! If he remembered and spoke of it now, how could she explain away her work at the tavern? What would Lady Arabella think of her then? As she proffered her hand, Topaz closed her eyes and prayed.

ELEVEN

TOPAZ felt the gentle pressure of Jason's fingers on hers and opened her eyes. Her heart was beating fast in alarm, but Jason merely bowed his head and said quietly, 'I am delighted to meet you, mistress.' When he straightened again Topaz saw there was a smile flickering behind his tawny eyes, but it did not reach his lips. Was it merely a smile of pleasure, or a mocking smile revealing that he knew only too well that she was but a tavern wench masquerading as a lady?

Whichever it was, Jason betrayed no other sign that he remembered their first meeting in the Nimble Rabbit. A serving maid entered, bearing a tureen of soup, and Lady Arabella signalled to Topaz to come and sit beside her, then she launched forth into a voluble description of her journey to her children. Sophie, sitting across the table from her mother, listened and nodded and asked questions from time to time, but Topaz realized to her dismay that Jason was not listening at all. His eyes rested on her throughout the chatter, and she felt confused with embarrassment. Eventually even his mother noticed his absorption.

'Now Jason, you haven't listened to a word I've been telling you! You haven't changed a bit during my absence, I see! Still you have eyes only for a pretty girl!'

Jason smiled. 'If you introduce me to so fair a maid and place me opposite her at supper, surely you could not expect me to ignore such an opportunity to feast my eyes, Mother?'

Lady Arabella's laugh trilled out. 'But you are to confine your admiration to your glances, my boy,' she said mock-chidingly. 'Topaz has been invited to join us as a companion for Sophie, not for you. You must find your own companions.'

Topaz did not see Jason's reaction to his mother's teasing, for her attention was caught by the sudden slight movement of the girl next to her. She looked up and saw Sophie looking full at her, for the first time since they had met. In her dark eyes there was a guarded look, not exactly hostile, but Topaz knew by the way she had stiffened that she did not welcome her mother's proposal.

Topaz smiled at the dark, thoughtful eyes by way of breaching her defences, but Sophie looked away quickly and engaged her mother again in conversation. She told her of their English friends who had called to visit her, and suddenly Lady Arabella interrupted her.

'Oh yes, now I remember! Sophie, do we know of a Mr. Barlow amongst the English people here in Rotterdam? A Mr. Charles Barlow, a merchant?'

Sophie placed her fork thoughtfully on the table and leaned her chin on her hand. A slight frown creased her white forehead. 'Barlow?' she murmured. 'No, I don't think so, Mother.'

Lady Arabella sighed. 'Pity. Topaz was enquiring after him, and I couldn't remember whether I'd come across the name or not.'

'Oh.' Sophie picked up her fork again and busied herself with her food. Topaz had the distinct impression that Sophie no longer cared about Mr. Barlow if it was only Topaz who wanted to know about him.

After the supper dishes had been cleared away by a pretty, flaxenhaired maid, Lady Arabella led them to sit on a green velvet couch by the fire. It was an elegant room, with green tapestry hangings embroidered in gold thread, and green smooth velvet covered all the chairs. Topaz felt sleepy by the warmth of the fire, and had only half an ear to the conversation. Lady Arabella was questioning her children about events in Rotterdam during her absence.

'The town is filling rapidly with yet more and more English people,' Sophie was telling her. 'You can feel the excitement in the air—everyone is certain the King will be restored any day now. Oh, Mother, won't it be wonderful to go back to London again? I can scarcely remember it, for I was but a child when we left.'

Topaz relaxed and enjoyed the warmth, not just of the fire, but of the close family feeling that absorbed the other three occupants of the room. She almost envied Sophie. How wonderful it must be to have such a mother and brother! At the thought of Jason, she turned her head slightly and looked across at him. She slid her glance quickly away again when she saw he was still watching her closely, and felt relieved when Lady Arabella suggested it was time for bed after their weary coach journey.

As she lay in the blissful comfort of the huge oak bed, warmed by the maid with a pan of coals before she climbed in, Topaz wondered yet again where Charles might be now. In her heart she felt sure she must be getting close to him—had not Sophie said all English exiles were flocking to Rotterdam and The Hague? Somewhere, some time, I shall find you, my love, she murmured. . . .

Charles brandished a letter under James' nose.

'Have you read what Mordaunt writes me? He is just back in Ostend from England, and he is convinced of Monk's support for me! What should I do, James? Shall I write to Monk at once and say I am ready to come the moment he gives the signal?'

James rubbed his chin thoughtfully. 'Like our old friend Hyde, I would suggest caution, Charles. Write by all means, offering your trust, but keep it vague. He is not the man to enjoy feeling he is being used.'

'Well,' said Charles reflectively, 'perhaps I should say something to the effect that I know he wants what is best for his country. . . .'

'A good move, yes, appeal to his patriotism.'

'And he must know that my heart is full of the same end.'

'He has no doubt heard tales of your behaviour over the years, Charles, and may believe you are fickle and shallow.'

'Then I shall tell him that whatever he has heard of me is false. I shall acknowledge his power over me—to do me good or harm in his position—because it will appeal to him that a King acknowledges his power.'

James nodded. 'Well, draw up a draft of the letter first along these lines, then see what Hyde and Nicholas think of it. It seems a reasonable enough move to me.'

Charles left James to his thoughts and returned to his chamber to pen the letter. His dark, handsome face creased in thought as he carefully phrased and rephrased the wording of what he considered the all-important letter. He could have been spared the laborious hour at the writing desk, had he but known that at the same moment two riders hurtled through the night at breakneck speed on their way to Brussels from Ostend. One of them, Mordaunt, ever-hopeful for the King's restoration, had just learnt wonderful news from the other, his friend, Sir John Grenville. Grenville had joined him at Dover just as Mordaunt was about to leave in a hired vessel, for Ostend, and he had been glad of Grenville's company when he learnt he too was on his way to the King. What he did not know until this moment was the reason for Grenville's visit.

Sir John Grenville came directly from General Monk to the King with the offer of restoration to the throne. Mordaunt was overjoyed, as he knew Englishmen everywhere would be.

Excited and deliriously happy, he and Grenville could not rest until they reached Brussels with the news. As they spurred on, Grenville told him what else Monk had commanded him to tell the King.

'To release the people from fear, Monk suggests the King should issue a free and general pardon to all, issued under the Great Seal, and grant liberty of conscience for all. Moreover, he considers it would be wise if the King should leave Brussels, which is in Spanish territory, at once, for England is still technically at war with Spain. King Philip might possibly detain him in Flanders if he knew of the negotiations, so we must persuade him to go to Breda or some other English possession for safety's sake.'

Three days after he had dispatched his letter to General Monk, Charles was playing hazard with James when he was urgently requested to attend the Chancellor Hyde in his chambers.

'What's afoot then, Edward?' asked Charles as he strode nonchalantly in, closely followed by James. His eyes narrowed in the dim light of the room and he made out the figures of three other men—there was Nicholas—and his friends, Grenville and Mordaunt! There must be news from England!

Charles suppressed the excitement that rose unbidden inside him. 'Greetings, my friends,' he said with a smile, holding his hands out to them. They both bowed, then Grenville straightened, smiled gently, and told him of General Monk's message. Then he produced the letter he himself had penned, memorized word for word from Monk's letter which he had been obliged to destroy, for safety's sake, before leaving Monk.

Heads clustered over the table, eagerly scanning the letter, and above them Charles stood, smiling, the eager excitement welling up inside him again. At last, after all these years, he was to be restored to his birthright!

Gradually the buzz and stir began to change to earnest discussion. The men drew chairs up to the table and began to go over the suggestions in the letter point by point. There was the question of land settlement which gave rise to a highly involved problem, the question of amnesty and the one of religious toleration. And, most important, the question of dealing with the murderers of his father, Charles I. This last one Charles decided to leave to Parliament to solve.

At length, after many hours' discussion, a declaration was drawn up, copies of which were to be sent to Monk, the Common Council, and both Houses of Parliament. And every man present agreed it would be best to take Monk's advice and remove the King from Spanish territory without delay.

Charles was exultant. He was so supremely happy he wanted to shout from the rooftops, but at this moment it would be extremely unwise. He must make his departure from Brussels appear casual at all costs, lest King Philip should suspect. He arranged that his brothers, James and Henry, should ride away first, and he should follow later. When he had seen his brothers safely away, he called on the Spanish governor and informed him he planned to visit his sister Mary at her court in Breda for a few days. This done, he went home to sleep.

He was awakened roughly in the small hours by Edward Hyde.

'Up, at once, Your Majesty! There is no time to lose—we must get you out of Brussels before daybreak!' he said quickly and with unwonted excitement.

'What's amiss, Edward?' Charles blinked against the candle-light in an effort to focus his attention.

'Galloway, the young Irishman, has just been to tell me that he has overheard that the Spanish governor plans to put a watch on you in the morning. He has seen the Governor's written orders—not on any account are you to be allowed to leave the town!'

Charles was instantly on his feet. By three o'clock he, James,

Grenville and a few servants were stealing silently out into the night and along the road to Antwerp. In Antwerp Mordaunt was awaiting them, and they journeyed on to Breda.

In the safety of Breda, Charles signed the declaration and put it into Sir John Grenville's hands to deliver to England, and Grenville and Mordaunt left for the coast at once. Then Charles sat back, contentedly, to await his destiny.

Life, Topaz found, was pleasantly smooth and carefree in Lady Davenham's household. For the first time in her life Topaz had no domestic duties to perform, and all that was expected of her was conversation and companionship. With Lady Arabella, not with Sophie, for Sophie politely but firmly declined to become closely familiar with Topaz as her mother was. In any event, she was too fully occupied with entertaining her own friends or going to visit them to be overmuch concerned with a companion who was not of her own choosing.

Whenever English visitors came, Topaz kept her ears open for a possible reference to Charles or to his colleague, James Butler. It was not very likely, she was forced to admit to herself, but one never knew. . . .

Jason, for his part, did not shun her company as Sophie did, but he was very withdrawn in his manner towards her. Frequently she caught him gazing at her thoughtfully, and always he looked quickly away or passed some lighthearted remark about the weather or the gay costumes he had seen in church on Sunday.

Topaz went to Mass alone, and making her Easter duties of confession and penance put her forcibly in mind of the last occasion she had done so. Only twelve months ago since that visit to the village church back at home, her pleading with St. Teresa for a sign—then the omen of the chicken. That was just before Charles had come into her life. Only a year ago? It seemed impossible that so much could have happened since then. She remembered how joyfully she had recognized the dead chicken's egg as a sign of good fortune; of that she had been convinced despite Hannah's doubtful fears. Was she still so pleased, so happy at the sudden change that resulted in her previously uneventful life?

Topaz hesitated for a moment. The ugly scene with Kaspar, Detlev's attempt to rape her, the degradation of the Nimble Rabbit, then the pain at the loss of her child—was it truly worth the eagerness with which she had welcomed the change?

Suddenly she saw clearly in her mind's eye the lost and weary Charles who had softened to a kindly, loving creature in her company, and the gentle dark-eyed looks of love he had lavished on her. She closed her eyes and quivered again as she thought of his touch, and the stirring vibrancy of his low voice when he spoke of love. Yes, oh yes! she cried inwardly, I am proud and happy I met Charles, whatever the cost, and I know we shall meet again! Somewhere, he too is waiting and hoping to find me, I know it!

Lost in such reverie one day in the library, Topaz looked up to see Jason leaning over a chair back and watching her silently.

'I did not see you enter, Jason?' she said, embarrassed at being caught deeply immersed in such intimate thoughts.

'You were in contemplative mood, Topaz,' he answered, and she saw the smile in his eyes flicker again. Was he mocking her again? Topaz felt angry. She wished she knew for sure whether he remembered her or not. As he did not speak further, she suddenly made up her mind to ask him outright.

'Jason?'

'Yes?' He came round the chair and sat down, crossing one velvet-clad knee over the other. 'What is it, Topaz?'

'Do you remember me?'

There was a pause. The only sound for a moment was the

crash of a log settling down among the ashes in the hearth. Jason was smiling broadly now.

'In the little Dutch tavern, you mean? Yes, I do, but I was beginning to think I must have been mistaken.'

'You recognized me instantly, did you not? Why did you not speak of it?' Topaz ventured.

Jason gazed floorwards thoughtfully. 'Even if it was not apparent then, it most certainly is now that you are a lady of breeding. Whatever reduced you to work in such a place, it was obviously not of your choosing, of that I am sure. I must confess I was a little dubious when you first arrived, and wondered whether you had duped my poor gullible mother.'

Topaz looked up sharply. 'Do you think still that I had some ulterior motive in coming here?'

'If you had, you have either discarded it or you are showing remarkable patience. I wonder which it is. . . .' He was still smiling evenly. Topaz felt like a poor fish that the fisherman was gently baiting and playing before suddenly hooking it and gutting it with his knife.

'I have no wish to dupe Lady Arabella, I assure you. She has been kindness itself to me,' she said stiffly.

'To be sure, she is always kind to everyone,' Jason agreed. 'But why are you here, Topaz? Whether tavern maid or cultured lady, what led you to come hither? Even though my mother invited you to be companion to Sophie, why did you leave your home and venture abroad alone?'

Topaz sat silent. She did not feel Jason truly trusted her, but she had spoken of her misfortunes to no one up to now, save Reverend Mother. Not even the warm-hearted Lady Arabella had learned her history yet—why should she tell this suspicious young man her reasons?

'I cannot tell you,' she answered quietly.

'Then I must be forgiven for believing you to be an adventuress, Fräulein,' he said gravely. 'A highly attractive one, it is true, but you are so reticent about yourself that it would seem you have something to hide.'

Topaz flushed indignantly. 'Even my sister,' Jason went on, 'seems not to care to make her relationship with you too close. Perhaps she too has reservations about you.'

Topaz's patience snapped. She rose quickly, her book sliding from her lap to the floor with a crash. Jason rose too. 'I care not how you feel about me, sir,' she snapped, 'nor your sister either. If you feel I am not to be trusted, I shall leave.'

She glared up at him and was angered by the amused smile on his face.

'And where will you go, Topaz? And if you did, my mother would never understand why you deserted her.'

Topaz felt bewildered. This man was enjoying his power over her. Again she thought of the cruel fisherman playing the doomed fish, and enjoying the delay.

Not trusting herself to speak again, and overcome as she was by unreasoning anger, she swept to the door and out, before Jason had time to open it for her.

TWELVE

RAINY April days changed into the warm promise of May. The air of suppressed excitement in Rotterdam became overt jubilation—it was certain now that the King was soon to be restored to his throne. Lady Arabella was ecstatic.

'After all these years, the poor boy is to regain his inheritance at last,' she said. 'Hardly a boy now though I fear—a grown man of thirty he must be, but he was but a boy of sixteen or so when last I saw him, before his poor dear father was so cruelly murdered.'

Sophie was less concerned with the King's rights than the imminence of their return to London. She busied herself with the arrangements for closing down the house in Rotterdam and transferring their luggage to The Hague port of Scheveningen, to be ready to board the earliest packet boat available. Topaz offered to help with the arranging, but Sophie brushed her offers aside.

Lady Arabella noticed nothing amiss between the two girls. In her own happiness she obviously thought everyone felt as warm and outgoing as herself.

'Topaz,' she said thoughtfully one morning as she and Sophie were supervising the packing of their gowns, and the maid bustled from the press to the hair trunks and back again, 'Have you decided whether or not you wish to accompany us to England?' For fear of being misunderstood she hurried on. 'Do not mistake me, my child, I shall be desolate if you do not come with us, but I would not wish to make you leave your own land to journey to foreign places if you do not feel you would be happy there. What would you like to do, Topaz?'

Sophie had stopped giving orders to the girl in order to watch Topaz's reaction. Topaz looked at Sophie, who looked sharply away. She was not going to receive any help in her decision from that quarter, Topaz reflected.

She hesitated a moment, pleating her skirt in her fingers. Then she saw Lady Arabella watching her hopefully. 'It is difficult for me, Lady Arabella,' she said in a small voice. 'Leaving Holland is no hardship for it is not my home—I am already far removed from my own home, both in time and distance. But I was engaged as a companion for your daughter, and it is for her to say whether she wishes me to continue in your company or not.'

Lady Arabella smiled with relief. 'I am sure Sophie finds your presence as amiable as I do, do you not, Sophie?'

Sophie shrugged her shoulders, very slightly, but Topaz saw the gesture. 'If you and Topaz wish it, I am content that she should come,' Sophie answered calmly.

'There, I knew she wanted you too,' said Lady Arabella with a smile of satisfaction. 'And if you are willing, Topaz, all is settled.'

Again Topaz hesitated. Sophie wanted her no more than Jason did, but Lady Arabella would be sad if she refused. And the other reason for going to England was undeniable. Charles, along with all the English people still in Holland, would undoubtedly be returning to London very soon. Had he not said it would be easy to trace him in London?

There was no longer any choice to be made. The way was clear.

'Lady Arabella, I shall be very happy to come with you, and I thank you,' she said simply. Beaming, Lady Arabella took her arm with one hand and Sophie's with the other, and led them downstairs to breakfast.

Later that afternoon Topaz was walking in the garden. Rounding a bend in the path through the shrubbery, she came across Sophie, basking in the sunshine, an open book beside her on the seat. It was too late to turn and retrace her steps, so Topaz advanced.

Sophie blinked up against the sunlight. Topaz came and sat beside her.

'Sophie,' she said quietly, 'I would not wish to disappoint your mother in any way, as she has been so kind to me.'

'That is one of her nicest failings,' said Sophie coolly, 'Helping lame dogs over stiles.'

Topaz ignored the slight. 'But I would not wish to intrude where I have no business to be,' she went on levelly. 'So if you—and perhaps Jason—would be happier without me. . . .'

'You cannot change your mind now,' Sophie interrupted her. 'You have promised my mother you would come, and she is delighted. What I would prefer is beside the point. What I *do* want, is that my mother should not be disappointed. So there is no need for further discussion of the subject. You are to accompany us to England and live with us in London as my companion. That is all.'

She rose as a sign that the discussion was at an end and with a faint semblance of a smile to Topaz—mocking again, Topaz wondered, like Jason?—she walked quickly away towards the house.

Topaz sighed. Her hand touched the book, still open on the seat. She picked it up and turned it over. 'A History of Philosophy,' she read. Strange reading matter for a young and lovely woman. As her mother had said, Sophie was very clever, and as a result would not tolerate fools lightly. That was no doubt what Topaz was to her—a feckless fool, reliant on the help of a generous woman like Lady Arabella.

And to Jason she was, it would seem, a schemer, a girl out for what she could get. Topaz sighed again. It was a bitter thing, to be so misunderstood. Only Lady Arabella loved her for herself, openly and with no reservation, and asking no questions. After all the misery of the past year, it warmed Topaz's heart to think of the kindly, loving creature, and she resolved she would go with the family to London, come what may, for the sake of Lady Arabella, and for Charles.

She picked up the book and walked slowly back to the house.

For Charles events were moving swiftly now. Admiral Montagu was coming to Scheveningen to escort him home. Accordingly he left Breda for the coast, and this time he travelled in triumph, in magnificent coaches provided for him and his entourage, no longer a fugitive stealthily travelling by night. Vast sums of money had been laid at his disposal by the States General, and Grenville had returned from England with ten thousand pounds in gold for him. It was incredible to see such a sum, and Charles had called his sister Mary to come and gaze at such an unbelievable sight!

In The Hague, Charles was acclaimed by multitudes of laughing people lining the streets, and welcomed by his aunt Elizabeth of Bohemia to her court. He sent word to General Monk that he would set sail for Dover, God willing, on Monday the 21st of May. From then on all his time was taken up by the royal round of ceremonies; there were delegations to meet and hear, scrofula victims, delighted to have a king again, came to be touched by Charles so as to be cured of the 'King's Evil', and there were interminable feasts and celebrations.

The climax came on Sunday night, the night before he was due to sail. Prince Maurice of Nassau and the States of Holland gave a state banquet in Charles' honour, and Charles revelled in the pomp and splendour of the occasion. The walls of the chamber were hung with cloth of gold, and light came from wax candles in huge silver candlesticks on the tables. At the high table, surmounted by an ornate gilded crown, Charles sat with Elizabeth of Bohemia on one side of him and his sister the Princess Royal on the other. He dined off plates of gold, and afterwards the whole set was presented to him.

Volleys of gunfire outside signalled a royal salute, and he knew people everywhere were merrymaking with fireworks and music throughout the night. Charles was proud and happy that his people were happy for him.

During the night Barbara was ushered into his chamber. The look on her determined little face was enough to dispel his happiness. He thought he could guess what she wanted.

'I shall, of course, accompany you on board the *Naseby* tomorrow, shall I not, Charles?' she said some time later as they lay entwined on the silken sheets. That was it, he thought, that was what she wanted; public recognition of her position as the King's mistress.

'I think it would be highly inadvisable, my love,' Charles murmured, stroking the mahogany red hair that covered her shoulders.

'Why?'

' 'Twill be a very formal and official occasion, and it would no doubt anger my more sedate subjects if they were to see you alongside my family.'

Angrily she flung him off and rolled over. Charles saw her shoulders heaving, and knew she was breathing deeply in anger. Soon it might turn to tears. Ah me!

He stroked the silky thigh, but it jerked away from him.

'You don't want me with you!'

He sighed. 'Of course I do, my kitten, you know I hate to be parted from you for a second.' His long fingers caressed her as smoothly as his voice did. 'But you know as well as I that it would not be wise for us to travel together. You must appear the dutiful wife, travelling with Roger.'

'Roger!' she snapped impatiently. 'The weak, dim fool!'

She rolled over, her deep blue eyes large and pleading. 'I want to be with you, my darling, please do not desert me!'

Charles took his opportunity and leaned over her, stopping her mouth. She relaxed a moment, then turned her head aside to murmur, 'Please!'

God! How her smooth voluptuousness tormented and satisfied him! 'One thing I promise you, my lovely—the first night I am in my own capital again, you shall be with me to share my joy. This I promise you,' were the last words he murmured into the pink ear before waves of ecstasy robbed him of speech.

During the night the wind rose, and by morning it was apparent that the rough weather and high seas would delay Charles' departure. But on Tuesday the sun shone and the wind dropped, and it was decided to set sail with the tide early on Wednesday.

All Tuesday night Charles heard the drums throbbing on the shore, and when he finally went down with his brothers and his sister and his aunt, he found a crowd of at leasty fifty thousand people who had been waiting all night on the dunes to see him leave.

His heart was full as he boarded the *Naseby* with Admiral Montagu. Thirty-eight great British ships waiting to escort the King home thundered a royal salute, and so did the Dutch cannon. The crowd on the sand dunes grew to over a hundred thousand as the morning wore on. Charles sat down to a farewell dinner with his family, then bid his aunt and weeping sister good-bye.

Brother James then went on board the *London*, and young Henry embarked on the *Swiftsure*. Charles renamed his ship the *Naseby*, the *Royal Charles*, and in honour of his family he renamed other ships after them—the *James*, the *Mary*, the *Henry* and the *Henrietta*.

At four o'clock, exultant, Charles set sail for England. Behind him he was leaving the poverty, the degradation and humiliation of all the years of exile. England, home and happiness lay before him.

Two days later he anchored at Dover, and General Monk was there to meet him. Gunfire from the ships and the fort roared a greeting, and a huge crowd covered the beach. Charles' eyes were dim with suppressed tears as he stepped out of the barge, and he knelt and thanked God for his safe homecoming. Then he rose and embraced Monk.

In a haze of bewilderment he was then led to Dover Castle and presented with a gold-clasped Bible before continuing his journey to Canterbury by coach with his brothers. But two miles out of Dover he could sit still no longer. He was longing to breathe fresh English air again. He called for his horse and rode out ahead of the coach to sniff the scent of thyme and recall . . . this was home, his England!

In Canterbury he was the guest of Lord Campden for the week-end. Here he had a foretaste of what was to come. Apart from greetings and presentations and conferring honours on his champions, he found himself inundated with complaints from royalist adherents about their ill-treatment and losses, and imploring his recognition of their loyalty by a present of either money or a position at Court.

Gradually Charles' patient good humour began to wane and he was relieved when Monday came and he was able to set off again towards Rochester. All the way along the route cheering crowds lined the roads, and Rochester itself was bedecked as for a carnival. He stayed the night with Colonel Gibbons, then on Tuesday, his thirtieth birthday, he rode triumphantly into London.

The citizens were mad with joy. Here, at last, was their 'Black Boy', home again after so long an exile. The sunlit streets were hung with tapestries and the fountains flowed with wine. Spectators crowded the wooden stands till they groaned and creaked under their weight. Morris dancers, with tabor and pipe, danced before the procession of soldiers on horseback, and bells rang out in jubilation while Charles rode bareheaded along the carpet of flowers his people strewed before him.

He rode erect, tall and slim, in a plain suit of dark cloth and a plume of scarlet feathers in his hat. Henry and James rode just behind him until at last they reached the Palace of Whitehall. Fourteen hours of travelling lay behind him. Charles was too exhausted by fatigue and emotion to attend the service of Thanksgiving in the Abbey that evening. He was obliged to hear the address from the House of Lords, and then he had to go to the Banqueting Hall to hear the oration of the Speaker of the Commons.

When the long address came to an end, Charles rose wearily to his feet. 'I am so weary,' he said, 'that I am scarce able to speak, but I desire you may know, that whatsoever may concern the good of this people, I shall be as ready to grant as you shall be to ask.'

Then he returned to Whitehall, and there he made his own private thanksgiving before he went to bed. Once in his own chamber, he suddenly remembered his promise to Barbara. 'The first night I am in my own capital again, you shall be with me to share my joy,' he had said. In the overwhelming events of day he had almost forgotten!

Charles sat on the edge of his bed. The Commons committee had indeed dealt handsomely by him when they had prepared his bedchamber. The rich velvet bed, embossed with gold and lined with cloth of silver, the great satin quilts and the down bolster, looked very inviting. Charles rubbed his sore eyes, irritated by the heat and dust of the day and longing for sleep.

It was no use. Barbara would never forgive him if he broke his promise to her. He had arranged for her to dispose of her husband and await him at the house of Sir Samuel Morland, and there she would be now, excited and full of anticipation. He knew only too well the rage of which she was capable if he disappointed her.

As he rode quickly towards Lambeth, Charles heard the bells of Westminster Abbey and knew his people and ministers were giving thanks for his restoration, just as he was slipping quietly away to the arms of his paramour. He smiled to himself. It was rather ironic.

THIRTEEN

IT was some weeks after the King and his entourage had left Holland before Lady Arabella could secure berths on the packet home to England.

Topaz was bursting with excitement as they embarked, and Jason seemed amused by the childlike joy with which she wanted to explore every part of the ship. He warned her laughingly that she might not be hurrying round with such bright-eyed eagerness soon, if the weather was not kind to them.

But the fair weather continued. Topaz stood with Jason on the moonlit poop and watched the Dutch coastline receding into the dark. Still the thrill of anticipation and hope leapt within her.

Next morning she rose and went on deck. Jason and Sophie were already standing at the rail.

'Look, Jason, look!' Sophie was crying, clinging to his arm and pointing. Her dark eyes shone and her face was alive with eager anticipation. Topaz's eyes followed her outstretched arm. There were the cliffs of the English coastline, and a little town nestling below the grey outline of a castle on a hilltop.

Dover! England at last! Still Topaz felt the thrill of excitement as the barge took them to the shore and she felt its bottom scrape on the shingle. After the customs officials had left them she could scarce eat the breakfast of boiled mutton at the inn, so anxious she was to continue the journey and see more of this country. Lady Arabella was no less excited.

'Come, children the coach awaits, let us be on our way,' she cried, pulling Sophie's arm and beckoning Jason who was settling the reckoning with the innkeeper. 'Come, Topaz, 'tis a glorious ride from here to Canterbury.'

And indeed it was. The day was so fine and clear Topaz could see the coastline of France plainly as the coach climbed the hill out of Dover. The dusty road stretched on for miles over open downs, the trees alongside swayed in the breeze off the sea, and the light summer clouds flew high. On they travelled, through apple and cherry orchards with fruit already ripe on the trees, till Canterbury came in sight, its old grey houses nestling in blossom-laden gardens around the narrow streets. How beautiful was England, Topaz thought. And how luxurious! The houses had glass in their windows, not shutters to draw across at night as at home.

Lady Arabella was still anxious to reach London as quickly as possible, so on they rode to Faversham and Rochester, through the lush Kent countryside. Topaz decided this was a country she could love without any effort. She could settle here happily with Charles.

At Rochester they dined at an inn near the bridge that crossed the Medway, then set off again immediately. Jason pointed out to Topaz the notorious spot called Gad's Hill, where robbers for a century or more had often waylaid travellers. Topaz shivered as she visualized this lonely spot on a dark winter's night, and was glad they were travelling on a bright summer's day.

Gradually, tired by travelling and the heat, the occupants of the coach dozed off to sleep. Topaz tried to keep her eyes open so as to miss nothing, but when Jason took her elbow and said, 'Look, Topaz, the Tower!' she realized she had been sleeping. She looked up and saw the grey, forbidding towers of the fortress rising stark against the city skyline, and alongside it, the Thames, flowing and gushing under the many arches of the bridge. Topaz's heart lurched with excitement again, just as the coach was lurching over the cobblestoned street. Dusk was beginning to fall, and she saw men lighting lanterns along the street. Not far from the river, the coach pulled into the courtyard of a large house.

'Home, Sophie, Belmont House, we're home,' cried Lady Arabella. It was a beautiful house, thought Topaz as she watched the women excitedly climb the steps of the stone staircase, lath and gleaming plaster, framed in oak, and the ornately carved upper storeys jutting out, as houses never did at home. And light glowed from the many mullioned windows.

Topaz followed the others inside. Despite the fact that the house had been closed up for many years, its very atmosphere seemed to breathe warmth and humanity to her as she heard Sophie running happily from room to room. Jason stood beside Topaz in the vestibule and smiled at Sophie's delighted cries.

'This was my room as a child,' she called down from the gallery. The excitement in her voice belied the chill reserve she had always shown hitherto.

Lady Arabella reappeared. 'Come child,' she said, leading Topaz upstairs. 'This shall be your chamber.' She indicated a chamber along the gallery, next to Sophie's. Topaz was amazed at its luxury—parquet floors, with deep fur rugs scattered about, and a huge fourposter bed, the posts of which supported an ornately carved tester, and from this fell magnificent drapes of deep green silk, exactly matching that of the draped curtains and hangings. Never before had Topaz slept in such comfort, and that night, despite her excitement, she slept soundly and long.

In the morning she found Lady Arabella and her children already up and talking in the pine-panelled library. Lady Arabella sat in a vast damask-covered chair, the red velvet curtains behind her shielding the sunlight from her face, but not from the silver candlesticks on the long oaken table, which threw the sunbeams back against the panelling. She smiled at Topaz and enquired whether she had slept well, then continued.

'We must get in touch with all our friends who have no doubt returned to London by now,' Lady Arabella was saying, 'and begin our social life anew. There is much to be done to make up for lost time—a husband to find for Sophie, for example,' she said, smiling benignly at her daughter.

'You can leave any marriage plans for me in abeyance, Mother,' the girl retorted, not unkindly. 'When I am ready I shall find one to my own choosing, if it please you.'

'Nevertheless, we must mix in society, as is expected of us,' replied her mother. 'We must issue invitations as soon as we have established which of our acquaintance are here. Jason, that will be your task.'

Jason smiled and nodded. To Topaz it was obvious that he would do anything to please his mother, however whimsical she might appear.

'Now, Sophie and Topaz, after we have eaten we must see to the ordering of food and whatever necessities have not yet been catered for, and when the house is in order, then we may see to ordering fresh clothes for us all. What we had is somewhat old and soiled, and new apparel will be essential. I shall enquire as to a good dressmaker for us.'

Immediately after breakfast Lady Arabella accordingly sent for the housekeeper and thrashed out these vital matters with her. Topaz found that no particular duties were expected of her for the time being, so she set out to investigate Belmont House and its gardens. It was a delightful house, and she could imagine Sophie and Jason as children, running around the spacious elm-circled lawns of the formal garden behind. Ornamental fountains, not yet restored to working order, decorated the paved terrace, and on a rustic seat at the far end she discovered Jason, playing with the housekeeper's cat.

'I am curious about you, Topaz, and no mistake,' he said flatly and with no preamble. 'Never once have I heard you speak of your family or your background, yet it is obvious from your every move and word that you are well-bred and nurtured. How came it about that I first saw you in that vile little inn? What circumstances led you to work in such evil squalor?'

Topaz hung her head and hesitated. Jason looked up from the cat and eyed her curiously. When she did not speak, he flicked a piece of silken thread just out of the cat's strained reach and added carelessly, 'You know, Topaz, it would be just as easy to tease you as this kitten here. Neither my mother nor my sister is aware of the degradation in which I first saw you, the filthy men pawing half-naked girls, and the fumes and stench of old ale and smoke, and neither, I believe, would be able to find any justification for your being there.'

Topaz's heart thudded in fear. 'You would not tell them, Jason?' He was watching her closely, and Topaz could see he took pleasure in seeing the pleading on her face.

'Will you not tell me then?' he asked, but Topaz did not like the levity of his tone.

'Not now. Some day, perhaps,' she answered slowly. 'Let it suffice for now that there was good reason.'

'Tell me of your family then, your parents.'

'They are both dead.'

'No brothers or sisters?'

'I have two sisters, both married and far away.'

'You are alone in the world then, Topaz?'

'As good as. The only friendship I have is that your mother gave me, and one other.'

'Another? Who is that? Someone whose track you have

lost, is that it? Is he in London, Topaz? Many foreigners are here in London now—perhaps I could help you find him?'

Topaz regarded Jason closely. The bantering tone was gone from his voice, and instead he sounded genuinely concerned for her. Was it possible he no longer viewed her with suspicion and was truly offering his friendship? The prospect warmed Topaz's heart.

'He is an Englishman—you may remember the name Charles Barlow—your mother enquired of Sophie when we were in Rotterdam whether she had heard of him. It is possible—indeed probable—that he has returned to London by now.'

'Barlow, Charles Barlow,' Jason repeated the name reflectively. 'No, I do not recall the name. What is his profession?'

'A merchant. I know not in what commodity,' Topaz replied, ashamed of her ignorance of her beloved Charles' way of life. She was half-ashamed of speaking of him thus to Jason, but if there was the slightest chance Jason could help her find him, no opportunity must be ignored.

'No matter,' Jason said cheerfully, 'if he is a person of any consequence in London, we shall undoubtedly come across him ere long.'

And as the hot days passed and more and more of Lady Arabella's friends and acquaintances came to visit, it seemed to Topaz that her kind friend did indeed know all the people of London. Topaz's heart lightened. Meeting so many people, it could be only a matter of time before someone appeared who knew Charles Barlow, merchant of London. . . .

Jason's attitude towards her now was far warmer and more friendly than Topaz had ever dared to hope. Even Lady Arabella noticed and smiled approvingly of the attention he paid Topaz, but Sophie's manner remained cool and distant. She declined all Jason's invitations to drive out in the carriage with him and Topaz to view London.

'Hyde Park today, I think,' Jason murmured one shimmering golden morning. ' 'Twill be hot and heavy again today, I fancy, and a drive in the park will whip up some small breeze to cool us,' and he whisked Topaz away to prepare.

London never failed to delight Topaz on each of their drives out to inspect it. Fine houses and elegant gardens contrasted sharply with the narrow cobbled streets and close-packed overhanging cottages on the south side of the river. Bustling markets and shrill street cries reminded her of the market town at home near Torwald, but the shops full of wonderful wares, and the fine-dressed ladies and gentlemen strolling in the sunlight were unprecedented in her experience.

Hyde Park revealed even more elegantly dressed creatures than she had yet seen. Fops and dandies twirled and made a leg to taffeta-draped beauties holding their parasols against the glare of the sun and smiling coyly at their escorts' attentions. Jason slowed the carriage as they circled the Ring, the better that they might view the company. Topaz gazed entranced.

A huge coach with a crest on its door stood waiting while a company of ladies and gentlemen entered it. Topaz saw a tall, bewigged man inclining his head to a lovely redhaired woman at his side, who was murmuring something to him. Two other men, resplendent in gleaming satin and frilled lace, stood by watching and chatting, and one advanced to touch the tall man's shoulder.

The tall man turned slightly, till Topaz could just see his profile. Her heart lurched. Surely it was he! At that moment their own carriage turned fully into the sunlight out of the shade of the trees and Topaz was dazzled. She could no longer see the face of the man as he helped his redhaired companion into the coach and climbed in after her. Jason stopped the carriage.

Topaz's heart was thudding in excitement. Was she mistaken, or was it really Charles she had glimpsed for a moment?

Jason smiled down at her and did not appear to notice anything amiss.

' 'Twere best we allowed His Majesty a clear way before we proceed,' he said. 'Did you know that it was our King and his brother and some friends who were taking the air?'

'His Majesty?' Topaz repeated dully. 'And his brother?'

'James, Duke of York. And I fancy the lady was Mistress Palmer that everyone speaks of.'

'And who else besides?' asked Topaz timidly. Had Jason recognized the third man, the one who looked so remarkably like Charles?

'There was Sir Charles Berkeley, close friend of the Duke, standing by the coach. The others inside I did not see,' answered Jason.

Sir Charles Berkeley? Topaz wondered inwardly, as she watched the coach lumber away into the distance. Could he have been her Charles? Had she seen aright? And if her eyes had not deceived her, what of his name? Had her ears deceived her long ago in Torwald, perhaps—she could have misheard the name Berkeley as Barlow. Foreign names were always a little odd.

But then Charles had told her he was a merchant, not a lord and a friend of the King's brother. It was possible he had assumed a false name somewhat similar to his own and claimed to be but a merchant for his own protection and for that of his royal friends.

Whatever the reason, if he was her Charles, Topaz felt sure his motives were good and honest. The problem now, she realized, was that if Sir Charles were indeed Charles Barlow, he was a gentleman of importance, and to reach him without embarrassing him might prove difficult. On the other hand, she knew he loved her, and when he knew of their child, he would want to marry her without delay.

If only she knew for sure whether she had found him or

not! Was it truly Charles she had seen, inclining his head in the graceful manner she remembered so well, to the lovely redhead at his side?

Jason recounted the incident to Sophie and Lady Arabella over dinner that evening.

'And the bewitching Mistress Palmer was among the company,' he concluded with a smile. 'And if the tales we hear are true, I doubt not His Majesty's taste.'

'That little strumpet!' Sophie snorted indignantly.

'My dear!' Lady Arabella remonstrated.

'Well she is, Mother! I have no sympathy with a creature with no brains, just a body that she uses to gain her own ends. And mark my words, that's all she's after, Mother—position, wealth, whatever she can wheedle out of the King in bed. Others have done it before her, and no doubt many others will again.'

'A royalist through and through,' remarked Jason jokingly. 'You would defend your King even against his scheming mistresses, would you?'

'Not I,' retorted Sophie. 'If he is fool enough—vain, weak and dull enough, to succumb to them—he must pay for his pleasures like anyone else. Any man as self-indulgent as he asks for all the punishment he will undoubtedly get.'

But Topaz was not listening to Sophie's heated criticism of the King. She was still wondering about the man in the park, and whether the sunlight had played tricks with her eyesight.

FOURTEEN

CHARLES floated on his back, letting the current carry him downstream, while his brother James swam energetically towards midstream. River bathing was a new pleasure he had only recently discovered, and it afforded a temporary relief from State cares to rise early and ride down to Putney or Battersea with James, before most folk were yet awake.

He struck one arm lazily, then the other, and headed towards the shore. Such a respite from care was all too brief, he reflected. In only three months on the throne of England all manner of unforeseen problems and irritations had arisen. His people wanted to see him continually; he was obliged to be constantly on public view, as when he performed the rite of touching for the evil, but demands for his services had grown so disproportionately that he had been obliged to curtail the event to Fridays only, and touching only two hundred at a time instead of the six hundred or so who had previously applied. He had also dined out frequently, and even when he dined at home in Whitehall, he was obliged to do so in public.

And the Lords had exasperated him greatly over the Indemnity Bill. The Commons had passed it quickly enough, but the Lords appeared to be particularly vindictive towards his father's killers, and continual debate had slowed the Bill almost to a halt. In the end he had been obliged to address the Lords on the matter himself, although he had agreed earlier to leave the punishment of the regicides to Parliament. He had pressed them in forthright terms to pass the Bill quickly, so that he could bring much-longed-for peace and security to his country as soon as possible. He had no wish to exact revenge on his father's murderers, but not until the end of August had they at last dealt with it, and to his relief, the Bill had been passed.

By then other matters had arisen to claim Charles' attention. Between visits to the theatre and an inspection of the East India fleet down at Gravesend, he had found it necessary to deal sharply with some who were carrying their newfound freedom too far. Duelling was becoming an almost everyday occurrence, and he was obliged to issue a royal proclamation expressly forbidding it.

Lesser, but equally irritating matters had angered him, such as the theft of his favourite dog, the cross-breed result of a greyhound and a spaniel, which he had brought home with him from Holland, and which had been accustomed to following him adoringly everywhere. Repeated advertisements in the *Mercurius Publicus* had had no success in tracing the dog. Damn the thieving villain! thought Charles. Cannot they even leave a man his pet dog, after robbing him of all else, including his privacy!

And then the letter from his mother, Queen Henrietta, had arrived, telling him of King Louis of France's request for Minette to marry his younger brother, the Duke of Anjou. Charles did not much care for the idea of Minette being entrusted to Monsieur's doubtful care, although his mother assured him that Minette loved him and was impatiently awaiting Charles' reply. Charles, feeling a trifle uneasy, had not yet given a direct answer. Louis was to send him envoys shortly to discuss the matter.

And now Mary, the sister he had not seen since their tearful parting on board the *Naseby*, had sent word to Charles that she intended to come and visit him in the autumn, leaving her young son in the care of the States General.

These were matters enough to occupy his mind for the moment, reflected Charles as he swam leisurely to the bank and stood there, dripping and shivering a little in the September dawn. Sometimes, just very occasionally, he thought wistfully of the days not long gone, when wenching and card playing were his sole worries, apart from the lack of money. And this latter problem had scarcely lessened now he was King, so paltry was the sum Parliament had granted him. He had even taken the occasion to comment on this to the Lords when they had passed the Poll Bill recently, to pay off and disband the Army, telling them forcibly how niggardly his house was kept, but it had had no visible effect on them. And now young brother Henry's sudden, strange sickness this week—it was all very disturbing.

'Come James,' he called to the distant figure in the water. 'Time passes and we must return.' Swift, strong strokes brought James quickly to the bank, and within minutes they were riding back to the cares and problems that awaited them in Whitehall. At least the masked Ball should afford further relief from care for a time, thought Charles hopefully. And the prospect of a night with Barbara lifted his spirits but little.

Crisp autumn leaves crackled underfoot as Lady Arabella, holding tightly on Topaz's arm, walked in the garden of Belmont House.

'I know it causes you pain, my child,' she was saying kindly, 'but in truth, a Catholic such as yourself is highly to be suspected by most of our people. Those who openly practise the Papist faith do so at their own risk.'

'But why?' asked Topaz. 'I mean no harm to anyone.'

'I know that well, my child,' replied Lady Arabella soothingly, 'But others who do not know you so well might well misconstrue. Since a long time past our people have distrusted Catholics, and sometimes with reason. 'Tis but fifty years since there was a fanatic named Guido Fawkes who, along with others, tried to blow up our Parliament.'

'But I would harm no one,' protested Topaz. 'I ask no more than to be allowed to go to Mass and Confession in peace.'

'Easier said than done,' replied Lady Arabella gently. 'Priests there are, but none who say Mass openly in church. They are forced to flee from one Catholic household to another, saying Mass where and when they can. I am in no position to help you find one, nor would it be safe for me and mine to do so. Do not misunderstand me, Topaz, I do not despise Catholics, but I cannot help you. And I would not advise that you profess your faith openly, for fear of some ignorant attack upon you.'

'Then what would you advise me do?' asked Topaz.

'The best advice I could give any Catholic woman alone, would be to marry a Protestant gentleman and thus gain his protection,' Lady Arabella said levelly.

Topaz started in alarm. So this was why Lady Arabella had sought to talk with her alone in the garden. She appreciated her benefactress's concern for her, but she did not wish to be married off conveniently. Not now, especially, when she believed she had glimpsed her own Charles at last.

Her fingers tightened defensively about the rosary in her pocket. She would be discreet about her faith, as Lady Arabella suggested, but continue to pray and act as she had always done. If none suspected, there would be no need to seek the protection of a Protestant husband. She wondered idly whether Lady Arabella had had any particular husband in mind for her, then thrust the thought from her mind as irrelevant.

Footsteps crunching towards them made Topaz and Lady

Arabella look up. Jason was striding purposefully from the direction of the house.

'Lady Katherine has called to see you, Mother,' he said, with a curt nod to Topaz.

'Lady Katherine?' repeated his mother in surprise. 'Is she returned from Europe?'

'It would seem she disembarked but a few days ago, and was anxious to see you again,' replied Jason with a smile.

Lady Arabella's face lit up. 'It must be months since we last met—at Cologne, I think it was. Forgive me, Topaz, dear.' She turned to Topaz and squeezed her arm warmly. 'I leave you to talk with Jason,' she said, and bustled away happily towards the house.

Jason turned and fell in step beside Topaz. 'Mother is not usually one for secrets,' he commented drily. 'I wonder what it was she was so anxious to discuss with you in private.'

'I can set your mind at rest on that matter,' answered Topaz quietly. 'She bade me practise my religion in private for my better safety.' She was about to go on, to say what else Lady Arabella had suggested, when she saw Jason's curious gaze. She hesitated. Jason was a Protestant, young, rich, and as yet unmarried. And as far as she knew, he had no particular fancy for any special woman.

Topaz kept quiet. If Lady Arabella had not planned a match between Jason and herself, Topaz did not wish to blunder by making him think she was setting her cap at him. Above all, she did not want to be misunderstood, now that she was so close to Charles.

Jason smiled and took her arm. 'That makes two of us who want to take care of you, Topaz, my mother and I,' he said, and to forestall any reply from Topaz he added quickly, 'Shall we return to the house? I fancy you might find Lady Katherine a most agreeable visitor.'

They walked back in silence, Topaz welcoming the warmth

and reassurance of his arm. Thank you, St. Teresa, she breathed, for giving me into the care of this kind family.

Lady Arabella was deep in animated conversation with her visitor in the library and did not notice their entrance. Jason drew Topaz to a seat in an embrasure. The sunlight streamed through the tinted glass and Topaz felt warm and contented as snatches of excited conversation drifted to her ears. She paid little attention, pondering as she was over Lady Arabella's advice and Charles' whereabouts.

'Yes, indeed,' Lady Katherine was saying, 'All set for the wedding, and then suddenly the bridegroom had a heart attack and died—just like that! Such a shock for the poor lady!'

'A relative of yours, did you say?' enquired Lady Arabella, her voice full of concern.

'No, no, but a very good friend. I used to visit her frequently in Munich during my travels.'

'Munich,' mused Lady Arabella. 'I had one or two friends in Munich—did I know her, by any chance?'

'Her name was Secker, Helena Secker,' replied the other. 'Widow of a merchant and still quite young. She was to have married a landowner from some town on the Dutch border—quite wealthy I believe, and the owner of a vast estate.'

Topaz heard no more. Secker—that was the name of the widow her stepfather Kaspar had gone to woo in Munich! It must be the same! Had Kaspar died of a heart attack? It seemed quite likely, in view of the unreasonable rages he sometimes flew into.

Topaz could feel little emotion for Kaspar's death. There had been no love between them in all those years, and hearing from Hannah how he had treated her mother had destroyed any feeling Topaz ever felt for him.

Hannah. She would be alone now at Torwald, if indeed she was still there. How much had she suffered from Kaspar's wrath after Topaz had left? But Kaspar was no longer there to harm anyone. Dully Topaz realized that now she was at last the rightful, undisputed owner of Torwald. The realization left her unmoved. She had no intention of returning to Germany, not now that she was almost knocking on Charles' door.

There was a lull in the conversation by the fireside, and Jason took the opportunity to draw her forward by the arm and introduce her to Lady Katherine. Lady Katherine smiled and bowed her head graciously in acknowledgement, while Lady Arabella smiled proudly.

'Have you yet had the opportunity of visiting Whitehall, my dear?' asked the stranger, after some preliminary questions about Topaz's country of origin.

'No ma'am, not as yet,' replied Topaz.

'Then you have not seen our dear sovereign,' continued Lady Katherine. 'You really should take the opportunity—he is such a fine, handsome man. He dines in public and touches regularly for the King's Evil, so it is not difficult to get a good view of him.'

'King's Evil?' murmured Topaz.

'A disease,' explained Jason. 'It is said it can only be cured by the touch of the reigning sovereign.'

'I am surprised, Arabella, that you have not yet presented Sophie or this young lady at Court,' Lady Katherine said reprovingly to her friend.

'An oversight I plan to rectify at once,' said Lady Arabella with a smile. 'As a matter of fact, I was going to speak of it today.'

Topaz felt a flutter of excitement. If she were to go to Court, there was a chance—a strong possibility even—that she could see Sir Charles Berkeley again, if he was indeed a close friend of the King's brother. And this time she would know for certain whether he and Charles Barlow were one and the same. . . .

With this thought to occupy her mind, all thoughts of

Kaspar's death and her right to Torwald were quickly dissipated. Sophie, however, was not so much excited at the prospect of being presented at Court as frankly bored.

'Do I have to, Mother?' she protested. 'You know I am hopeless at idle chit-chat and polite gossip. And the thought of being entertaining to all those elegant fops and womanish dandies bores me to distraction.'

'But my dear, it is expected of us,' replied her mother. 'I was presented at the Court of our dear King's father when I was much younger than you, but in your case, alas, it was not possible. It was by means of Court visits that I met your father,' she added persuasively.

'That settles it,' said Sophie decisively. 'I do not intend to go there husband seeking.'

'But there are men of letters and of great learning there,' her mother said softly. 'It is well known King Charles is a patron of the arts and of the sciences. Why, I believe he even has his own laboratory in the palace.'

Sophie remained silent for a time, musing over her mother's words. To Topaz it was evident that Lady Arabella had a subtle manner of persuading others to her own point of view, and that Sophie would eventually agree, perhaps outwardly unwilling, to be presented. Jason apparently was thinking the same thing, for he tipped Topaz a broad wink and smiled.

'And you, Jason, shall come too,' said Lady Arabella turning to him. 'In view of the love our late king bore your father, it is possible His Majesty may be prevailed upon to find some position for you.'

Jason looked at her in astonishment. 'But I have no wish to have a position, Mother,' he said. 'And there is no necessity —we do not need more money.'

'Perhaps not,' replied Lady Arabella firmly, 'but it will be good for your soul to do an honest day's work. You cannot spend your life simply gazing at the flowers of the field and admiring their beauty. You must prove yourself worthy of one.'

And with these words she swept out of the library, leaving a whiff of musky perfume in her wake. Did Topaz imagine that hint of a smile as she passed her? She looked up at Jason, and seeing he was looking hard at her, she dropped her gaze quickly, covered in confusion. Oh no, let him not think his mother was matchmaking the pair of them! It was unthinkable! Jason was a tolerant, easy-going enough fellow, and anxious to please his mother, but if he felt that she and Topaz were plotting to manœuvre him, Topaz might lose his newly-won friendship completely. She must rid him of this absurd misconception as soon as possible!

FIFTEEN

In a vast, gloomy chamber in Whitehall, James Butler, Marquess of Ormonde, Grand Master of the Royal Household, sat upright before the fireplace, watching the pale, thoughtful face of the young man opposite him, sprawled in a deep velvet chair.

'Come, Charles, it is your move,' he said, indicating the chess board between them. Charles murmured something indistinct and slowly uncurled and leaned forward over the table.

His eyes were still sombre and his mood thoughtful as he stretched his hand tentatively towards a piece, picked it up, hesitated, then slowly replaced it in the same position.

'I am sorry, James, my mind is straying elsewhere and not on the game tonight,' he said quietly.

James sat back, flexed his shoulders and sighed. 'You are in check, and inside three moves it will be checkmate unless you put your mind to it,' he said, 'and in other times such a position would be a challenge to you.'

'I concede you the game. Give me more wine,' sighed Charles, and as James poured the amber liquid into his pewter tankard, Charles toyed idly with a white pawn. 'It seems to me often that my life is like a game of chess, you know, James. Political manœuvres drive me relentlessly hither and thither whether I will it or no. Like the pressure that is put on me now to take a wife and to exact revenge from my father's murderers. It is odd, is it not, that I, the King, am but a pawn in many matters?'

James picked up the White Queen and fondled it. 'But the

White King has a bonny Queen to comfort him and soothe away his cares,' he said with a smile.

Charles snorted. 'Barbara? Soothe me? Never! She has the abrasive effect on me of a flint on a tinder box, inflaming me either to passion or to anger! But you are right in saying she is the Queen, James, the all-powerful piece on the chess-board, swooping and seizing whatever her heart desires.'

He paused, and James knew he was thinking of the many demands Barbara had already made upon him for gowns and carriages, a mansion and servants. Soon it would be a title, as befitted her position as the King's mistress.

'She has me in thrall, and well she knows it,' murmured Charles. 'In thrall to her magnificent body. I' faith, what a woman! She has the body of an angel, and the soul of a devil!'

'What, then, are these other pawns?' asked James, picking up scattered pieces from the board. 'The many other, lesser, mostly forgotten women who have crossed your path?'

'They are not forgotten,' said Charles firmly. 'I can remember all, well, most of them. Not by name, perchance, but they succoured me in my hour of need, and for that I remember and thank them.'

'Some of the King's pawns have remembered you, and already some of them have come hither to claim payment,' James reminded him.

'Well I know it,' groaned Charles, 'And my coffers are yet the more depleted.'

'Then an advantageous marriage to a bride with a handsome dowry might not be such a bad notion after all,' murmured James, packing the chess pieces away in their box, 'and we can but hope that no more of the King's forgotten pawns will appear.'

Topaz stood at the mullioned window of her chamber, watching the swirling russet leaves falling from the elms.

Suddenly there was a knock at the door, and a pink-faced Lady Arabella, her eyes ashine with excitement, swept in.

'Topaz, my dear, I have news!' she cried. 'Where is Sophie? She must hear, too!'

'She is in her chamber, I believe,' replied Topaz.

Lady Arabella hastened to the oak-panelled door that connected this room with Sophie's. She pulled the knob, but it did not yield. As long as Topaz had been here she had known the door to be kept locked, on Sophie's side.

'Sophie, Sophie, open the door,' cried Lady Arabella, and in a few moments the scraping sound of a bolt being drawn could be heard. 'Why do you bolt the door?' asked Lady Arabella. 'It was never locked before.'

'I prefer privacy,' remarked Sophie coolly.

Lady Arabella did not pursue her reasons, but went back instead to her news. 'Your presentation at Court has been arranged,' she said triumphantly. 'It will be next week, when His Majesty is to hold a grand masked ball, and we shall all attend it!'

She glowed with pride as she surveyed the girls, then her manner changed when she realized their lack of enthusiasm. 'Come now, surely it is a thrill to be going to Whitehall, to see His Majesty face to face! New gowns!—We must all order magnificent new gowns such as the Court has never seen before! And shoes, and fans—come, there is so much to be done!'

She bounced away again towards the door, and Sophie hurried after her, as though to convince her she really was enthusiastic about the great occasion, thought Topaz. As for Topaz herself, there was no denying the deep inner excitement she felt mounting inside her. Surely at Whitehall she would see Charles!

Later that day she asked Lady Arabella as casually as she could manage who else might be present at the ball.

'Who else, my dear? Why, everybody—everybody who is anybody in London will be there!' Lady Arabella cried in ecstasy. 'Oh, what a wonderful evening it is going to be! We must all take great pains to look our very best. We shall catch all eyes with our stunning beauty,' she said laughingly, but there was no hiding her open admiration for Sophie's dark beauty.

'And of what use is a fair face?' demanded Sophie. 'It serves only as a barrier. Men are so taken with it, they look no further for one's qualities. Better by far to be plain, it would seem.'

'Nevertheless, I would have you shown in your true colours at the ball, 'Tis a pity one must go masked,' observed her mother. 'No matter, everyone will unmask at midnight, and then all shall know what a lovely creature you are. 'Twill not be long until suitors are flocking to our door, I think, especially since there are two beauties here,' she added, her plump arm encircling Topaz's waist. 'Now, let me see—green, I think for you, Sophie—emerald taffeta. And for you, Topaz——' she held Topaz at arm's length and looked her critically up and down, 'for you, amber velvet to match your honey-coloured hair. Yes, I think so. Do you not agree, Sophie?'

Sophie shrugged her shoulders. 'Choose what you will, Mother. It matters little to me.'

But for all Sophie's indifference, Topaz waited impatiently for the day of the ball to come, and at last it dawned, misty and dull. All day she was in a fever of excitement for the evening to come, brushing her hair till it shone like burnished gold, pinching her cheeks to make them glow, and admiring the magnificent amber-coloured gown that lay ready, draped over a chair. If, as she longed, she were to see Charles again tonight, he must find her as lovely as when he left.

As dusk fell, she helped Sophie into her brilliant emerald

gown, and brushed her long fair hair and looped it with silver ribbons. Sophie looked beautiful, and she knew it, thought Topaz, for her cheeks were flushed and her eyes gleaming as she turned from the mirror.

'Come, let me help you now,' said Sophie, taking Topaz's arm and leading her to her own chamber. Topaz felt like a queen, sitting on a stool, the luxurious gold velvet gown falling in thick folds about her. Sophie's deft fingers braided and looped her thick hair with gleaming gold ribbon, then she stood back to admire her handiwork.

'There, you look ravishing,' she said curtly, then turned and swept from the room. Topaz stood up and advanced to the mirror. The sight almost took her breath away. With the froth of lace at elbow and hem she looked truly regal. Charles would be proud of her this night indeed!

The coach clattered over the cobbled streets westwards towards Westminster. Lady Arabella was talking excitedly to Sophie, but Jason sat withdrawn and silent in the corner. Topaz looked out of the coach window and watched the close-packed buildings in the narrow streets, and the urchins running barefoot between the puddles of mud and dung to leap on the running board. The coachman whipped up the horses to a gallop and left the ragged beggars far behind, and the coach's occupants were jolted unceremoniously about.

Finally they drew up before an arched gateway into a massive red-brick building. Jason helped the women down, then they all picked their way carefully through the mud, anxious lest they spoil their fine new slippers. They passed quickly through a maze of passageways and arched gateways, through halls and apartments where other masked people were pressing, laughing and carefree, until they came at last into a vast, crowded gallery.

'The Stone Gallery,' murmured Lady Arabella. 'It must be twelve years since I was here last.'

Topaz was overwhelmed by the enormous size of the place—hundreds of feet long, and with huge portraits along the walls. Crimson velvet drapes covered all the doors, some of which, Lady Arabella told her, led into His Majesty's own private apartments. And a myriad crowd of magnificently gowned ladies, elegant gentlemen, men in ornate uniforms and liveried servants seethed excitedly, laughing, flirting and exchanging the latest gossip. Topaz gazed, fascinated. A tall gentleman in a gold-buttoned surcoat and beribboned breeches was gazing back at her equally fervently from behind his fringed mask. He broke away from the group he was with and pushed his way towards her, his eyes never leaving her face.

Topaz felt embarrassed and turned to Jason and the others—but they were not there! Somehow in the crowd they had moved on without her—they were gone! She ducked quickly through the crowd, away from the pursuing dandy, alarm rising within her. There was no sign of the others in the throng. Which way had they gone?

She blundered on to the end of the gallery, and through the draped double doors. She heard the laughing jests and felt the restraining hands, but brushed them aside and hurried on. Suddenly, without the protection of her friends, she felt very vulnerable.

Sir Edward Progers, Page of the Backstairs, knocked discreetly on the door of the royal bedchamber in Whitehall, and glided in quietly in answer to the summons.

His Majesty the King stood tapping his forefinger impatiently on the spine of a leather-bound book in his hands. He was already dressed and masked for the ball.

'Well? Will she come?' he demanded.

The valet coughed discreetly, then murmured, 'My Lady Palmer bids you find another toy for your amusement this evening, Sire. She will be unable to attend.'

'The devil she does!' barked Charles. 'Damn the witch for her insolence! Does she think to force my hand by playing fast and loose with me? Thinks she that I will sit and brood with jealousy while she amuses herself with some other fellow?'

He turned sharply and looked out of the window across the river, his dark face clouded and vexed. Progers stood silent, awaiting further commands, too well-versed in His Majesty's ways to attempt to answer his rhetorical questions. Eventually Charles turned again, and Progers saw with relief that the sunny smile had returned to his handsome face. He leaned down to caress the spaniel fawning at his feet.

'Well, two can play at that game, Progers,' he commented drily. 'My lady will not be so pleased to discover I ignored her tantrum and did as she bade me. Find me another toy for the night, Progers—a quiet, undemanding creature, fair of face and form, but preferably a face that is new to me. I am of a mind for novelty tonight, and there is no novelty in my lady's rages.'

Progers bowed and withdrew. Ah well, he must go down and rejoin his guests, Charles reflected. To be in company was better than being left alone to brood, but he was well aware that many of the guests' protestations of love and loyalty were only a preamble to demands for recompense in some form. He found himself becoming more and more suspicious of his flattering courtiers' motives, always looking for the barb hidden within the bait.

He lifted the spaniel and placed it on a chair, then crossed the chamber and opened the door. With or without Barbara, he must go down, he thought, then with a prick of irritation he slammed the door after him. Blast her, trying to hold him to ransom! Tonight he must have a gentle, sympathetic creature. And after months of Barbara's animal sensuality, almost savage in its devouring greed, he welcomed the prospect of having to seduce a reluctant woman slowly and with finesse.

After wandering about for some time Topaz found herself back again in the Stone Gallery, and still there was no sign of the Davenham family. Alarm was beginning to develop into real panic as admiring arms crept about her waist as she passed, or marauding fingers clutched at her bodice, and it was with a fierce wave of joy that she caught sight of Jason's tall, fair head above the throng.

'Jason, oh Jason!' she cried with relief, and all but fell into his arms.

'Topaz! Where have you been?' he demanded, his face dark as he held her at arm's length. 'My mother has been distracted looking for you! Come!' he said sharply, and strode away, leading her firmly by the hand. In the ballroom he stopped, and after looking around above the many heads, he turned to Topaz.

'Bide you here and do not stir till I return,' he said crisply. 'I shall go find my mother and Sophie and then come back,' and with that he strode away.

Topaz sat on a velvet-covered couch and waited. She could see little of the chamber because bodies pressed in on her from all sides. She caught a glimpse of the masked and bewigged gentleman who had scrutinized her earlier in the Stone Gallery, but he quickly disappeared in the crowd.

Minutes passed. Topaz grew anxious and stood up, the better that Jason might see her, and as she did so, a tall, masked gentleman in bottle green velvet with a gold sash confronted her. He smiled, and said to his companion, 'You may go, Progers,' and the man from the gallery bowed his head and disappeared again.

Topaz's senses were stunned. The man in green was more than familiar to her. The smile and the voice—it was undeniably Charles! Despite the mask she could see the long, straight nose, the full lips, the warm, dark eyes, smiling and amused. Charles! My beloved Charles, after all this time! her heart sang, and she smiled. Then a thought crossed her mind. Had he also recognized her, despite the mask?

'Madam, will you dance?' The low, vibrant voice quickened all her senses into life again.

'With pleasure, sir,' she replied, and put out her hand. Oh, the joy and the exquisite pain when his hand touched hers! Could he not sense the vibration, too? He must remember—and so know her.

He led her for a few steps, then stopped. 'I fear it is somewhat hot and crowded in here. Shall we sit and talk instead? There is an alcove here,' and without waiting for her answer he led her to a secluded corner, curtained and magically left clear and uncluttered. He handed her to the sofa, then sat beside her. Topaz's heart almost forgot to beat in the excitement of being reunited with him at long last.

'You are a newcomer to our Court, are you not?' he enquired courteously.

'My first visit,' replied Topaz. Did he not know her? For a moment she felt a pang of bitter disappointment but then, remembering how long they had been parted, that she was masked, and that Sophie had said everyone was to unmask at midnight, she felt a glow of pleasure beginning to spread. Until midnight she could enjoy the sight of his wonderful, handsome face secretly, and the pleasure of talking to him, and then when the clock struck, she would savour his astonishment when she revealed her face.

'Are you with company?' he enquired, and again Topaz thrilled to the deep velvet quality of his rich voice.

'With Lady Arabella Davenham, my benefactress, and her son and daughter,' she replied gravely enough on the surface, but her emotions were turbulent beneath.

'I see.'

He talked to her for some time, quizzing her gently about how long she had been in England, and whether she found London to her liking, when somewhere in the distance a clock struck. Midnight already! thought Topaz. Immediately there was a cry echoing round the chamber from the multitude of throats. 'Midnight—unmask, unmask!' they cried, and then there was a babble of laughter and delighted shrieks as guests finally discovered who their partners were.

Charles smiled and pressed her hand. 'It is time to reveal ourselves,' he murmured, and reached up and unfastened his mask, letting it drop on his lap. Topaz gazed at his face in rapture. Oh my love, she cried inwardly, my precious, beloved Charles! Then she saw with dismay that his face bore signs of fatigue and worry, and felt deeply concerned. Oh my love, time has not treated you kindly either, she reflected sadly.

Then she brightened. But we are together again at last and I shall help to lift the load from your shoulders as best I may. She saw he was watching her curiously.

'Come, little one, it is your turn to unmask,' he reminded her gently. Shyly Topaz reached up and undid the fastening, her heart bounding in anticipation. Slowly she lowered the mask, and looked at him, smiling and expectant, awaiting the glow of recognition on his grave, dark countenance.

Charles lifted a long finger and stroked her cheek, and a slow smile played round his lips. Topaz hardly dared to breathe. 'You are indeed a beauty, little one,' he murmured. 'I am grateful you thought fit to grace our Court with your presence. Never before, I swear, have I beheld such fair, glowing beauty.'

As he dropped his hand to cover Topaz's hands, clasped tightly in her lap, Topaz's heart stopped beating altogether. The velvet drapes, the light from the torches, and his face swam hazily before her staring eyes. He did not recognize her! He knew her not! After all his protestations of love in the April sunlight, he did not remember her!

Charles, whom she had crossed half Europe to find, did not even recall the glorious, intoxicating week together that had been the climax of her life!

Suddenly Topaz felt violently sick, whether with shame or grief she knew not. A thought flitted across her mind, and she clutched at it desperately like a drowning man. Perhaps he was only teasing her—had he not often been gay and mischievous that week? And his name—Barlow or Berkeley—indicated he was perhaps given to practical joking. She gathered her wits and looked at him again.

He was still smiling gently and playing with her fingertips. In a moment he would throw back his head and laugh to show he was teasing her—surely?

Charles slid his hand slowly up over her wrist and elbow, then crossed to her frilled, low-cut bodice. His fingers made her flesh tingle with the thrill she remembered so clearly. He *must* know her—why did he tease her so?

'Charles,' she murmured timorously.

'Yes, my angel?'

'Do you remember me?'

Her words had an unexpected effect on him. He jerked his hand quickly away from her breast and looked her full in the face, his black eyes wide and incredulous.

'Madam, forgive me,' he said jerkily, as though embarrassed and ill at ease. 'Do you mean we have met before? I find it in my heart to doubt it, for I swear I could not forget such beauty.'

Topaz's breath caught in her throat in gasping sobs. He did not know her! Her head swam, and as she sank slowly to the floor, she saw his concerned face bobbing over her, then nothing. . . .

SIXTEEN

BLURRED faces greeted her eyes when Topaz came to her senses. Voices too—and among them, Charles' clear voice, demanding wine and a physician.

'Who is this child?' he was saying. 'I know her not—does anyone know her name?'

Topaz felt so sick with shock and disbelief, she scarcely heard Lady Arabella's voice in reply.

'It is Fräulein Birke, my protégée. I fear the excitement has been too much for her,' she said, laying a cool hand on Topaz's brow. 'Poor child, she was separated from us in the crowd, and no doubt was very frightened. Fear not, Topaz, I am here. We shall be home directly.'

'Allow me, madam,' said Charles' deep voice. 'My coach is at your disposal. I shall order my coachman to take you home immediately.'

'Your Majesty is most kind, but it will not be necessary,' Lady Arabella replied. 'I have my own coach—Jason, would you tell Hackett to bring it to the Holbein Gate at once?'

Topaz struggled to sit upright. Were her ears deceiving her? How had Lady Arabella addressed Charles? She saw Jason disappearing through the throng, and someone put wine into her hand. After a sip, almost unwillingly, she turned her eyes to Charles. He was no longer smiling, but his face was full of grave concern.

'How fare you now, Mistress Birke?' he said gently. 'I trust you are feeling better?'

Topaz could not trust herself to reply. His concern was only that of any man for a stranger—and this was the man who had sworn undying love for her when he got her with child in the fields of Torwald.

'Who is she?' he had said. Who is she? Topaz was numb. She felt herself led away from the chamber, more carried than led by Jason's strong arm. On the homeward journey in the coach she remained silent, too sick and numbed to speak, until she remembered Lady Arabella's words to Charles. Had she imagined it, or did Lady Arabella call him 'Your Majesty'? She had to know the answer.

'Indeed, child, did you not know it was the King himself?' said Lady Arabella in shocked surprise. 'But of course—you were missing when I presented Sophie to him—how could you know?'

Oh no! Topaz's mind refused to accept yet more bitterness. Never once had he shown in any way that he was of royal blood; a merchant, he had said, and as a merchant she had loved him all this time. But the King of England! It was incredible—impossible! That sad-eyed, lonely youth, wandering Europe friendless and melancholy, who had been so glad of her company and her love—he could not be the King!

But she had seen with her own eyes and recognized her Charles. And he was the King.

As she lay in her enormous bed, tossing and turning, another thought overwhelmed her. If Charles was a king, then the tiny scrap of flesh she had given birth to in a faraway convent was a royal child. She had given birth to a king's dead son. For the first time in months Topaz wept anew for the child she had lost.

She still could not believe the dreadful truth—that in all the last year and a half all her thoughts and hopes had been centred on a man she adored, and who had completely wiped her from his mind. It had been her belief in his enduring love that had kept her buoyed up throughout all those months of travel and misery, and in one night her illusion was shattered. To add to her misery, she had to discover he was no mere merchant but a monarch. Gone now were her dreams of happy marriage.

Perhaps she could take some crumb of comfort from the fact that she had been loved by a king—but to what end, if she was so unimportant to him he had immediately forgotten her? There was no comfort to be found anywhere, no matter how hard Topaz reflected on the affair. She had to face the truth. She had been but a moment's fancy to a fickle, shallow man.

No, no, not my Charles! In everything he did and said that week he showed he was far from shallow! Her love for Charles screamed abuse at all that her reason told her.

Finally, tortured with grief and exhausted, she fell into a restless sleep. Hours later she was awakened by a scraping sound, and she sat upright. The bolt on the connecting door to Sophie's chamber was being slowly and deliberately drawn. Then the door opened, and she saw Sophie, caught in a shaft of moonlight from the high window.

'Topaz, are you sleeping?' Sophie whispered.

'No, I am awake. Come in,' Topaz replied. Her head ached and her throat was parched and sore. Why was Sophie, who never sought her company, here, and in the middle of the night?

'I heard you sobbing and crying out,' Sophie told her. 'I thought perhaps it was some dreadful nightmare and it were best to waken you. Were you dreaming, Topaz?'

'I do not remember, but it was kind of you,' said Topaz with stiff, dry lips. Sophie sat tentatively on the edge of the vast bed and peered at her in the gloom.

'What is it? Is something troubling you?' asked Sophie, and

Topaz knew it was an effort for the other girl to ask. 'If there is aught amiss, perchance I could help,' she said.

Topaz turned her hot face into the coolness of the pillow. 'Naught that you can alter, Sophie,' she murmured.

'Forgive me, I do not wish to intrude on your privacy, but I am concerned, and I know my mother would be distressed if she thought aught was troubling you. You—you can tell me, if you wish.'

'Thank you, but no,' Topaz said firmly but indistinctly into the pillow. Sophie rose at once.

'As you wish. I only wanted to help,' she said stiffly.

'I am grateful—but some other time, perhaps,' muttered Topaz. 'No more tonight—for pity's sake, do not ask me to talk of it tonight.'

Her misery lay like a leaden weight on her body after Sophie had gone, and Topaz tossed and turned for a long time before she fell into a fitful sleep until dawn. As she dressed, still the feeling of empty torpor filled her. With pounding head and heavy-rimmed eyes she went down to the library. An animated Sophie was talking to her mother.

'Sir Richard is such a charming man, Mother, so earnest and intellectual!'

'And handsome,' commented Lady Arabella drily.

'That's beside the point!' retorted Sophie. 'It is his mind I admire—and I think he was somewhat impressed by mine, too.'

'I am glad you have found one man to your taste in London,' observed Lady Arabella. 'I take it you would have no objection to his coming to my little soiree next week?'

Sophie's smile of pleasure changed quickly to a look of concern when she saw Topaz standing quietly in the doorway. Lady Arabella hurried forward, clicking her tongue with annoyance.

'My dear child, you should not be out of bed! You need to rest and recover your strength.'

'I am well, Lady Arabella, truly I am,' Topaz said. ' 'Twas but the crowd and the lack of air that caused a fit of the vapours.'

Lady Arabella looked reassured. 'Have you eaten breakfast?' she asked.

When Topaz shook her head, she bustled out. Sophie crossed to the damask-covered seat in the window embrasure and sat silent.

Topaz looked at her, thoughtfully. Strange, she could feel nothing, neither for Charles nor for the friends who cared about her. It was as if someone had turned off the tap of her emotions. Sophie had made the first sign of friendship during the night, and Topaz was too numb to feel any reaction. She was well aware that the girl was waiting now to see whether she would make any move to meet her friendly overture, but she was so numb, so frozen, she was unable to say a word. And when Lady Arabella called her to come and eat, she turned silently and left. Sophie was still sitting gazing out of the window.

Charles sat hunched in a chair by the embers of a fire, his favourite dog at his feet rolling over and pleading with huge, eloquent eyes for her belly to be tickled. But for once her master did not respond.

Charles felt so shocked and saddened he had sent everyone away. His young brother Henry's sickness, from which he had appeared to be recovering so well, had suddenly worsened and he had died the same evening. That was five days ago, but Charles could still scarcely believe it. So young—hardly twenty years of age—and hitherto so healthy. Smallpox, the physicians had said. It sometimes carried people off with this unexpected suddenness. And James, his other brother, had gone down to the coast to meet Mary arriving from Holland. If he had already put to sea, it would be some time before the sad news reached him, and Charles knew what a terrible shock it would be both for him and for Mary, too.

A knock came at the door. Charles made no answer. He had told them all he wished to see no one. Another knock. After a pause the door opened and Progers entered.

'Sire, forgive me. . . .'

'Go away.'

'But Sire, His Royal Highness the Duke of York is returned.'

Charles looked up. 'Let him come in.'

Progers went out, and after a moment James strode into the chamber, still booted and wearing his travelling cloak. He spoke not a word, but gripped his brother's arm in mute mourning. Charles felt too choked to speak, and it was some moments before he let go of his brother's hand and sat down.

'Have you eaten?' asked Charles, seeing James' mud-stained clothes. He must make an effort to behave civilly even if it was the middle of the night.

James brushed the question aside and asked, 'How was it, Charles? They tell me it was the pox—did he suffer?' He flung his cloak across a chair.

Charles shook his head. ''Twas very sudden. In this at least God had mercy on him.' He asked about Mary.

'The ship is held in port still because of bad weather,' James told him, 'but she will be here soon.'

James looked out of the window at the lights flickering on the river. There was a long silence. His back still towards Charles, James cleared his throat and spoke. 'It would seem that the old adage about troubles never coming singly is indeed true,' he commented.

Charles grunted agreement.

'Charles, I regret bitterly having to broach another matter

with you at a time like this, but it is imperative I talk with you.'

Charles did not speak. If, by the sound of James' voice, it was more trouble—financial difficulties or a personal matter like a troublesome mistress—then Charles did not want to hear it. Had he not got enough to contend with as it was? James still had his back towards him.

'Well?' said Charles eventually, his curiosity overcoming his resentment.

'Charles, how would you feel about my marrying a commoner?' James turned to face him.

Charles looked at him in disbelief, then laughed, a curious, hollow, unmirthful laugh. 'Dammit, man, why bother me with mad hypotheses at a time like this? Don't tell me you've got a wench with child and feel constrained to make an honest woman out of her! You've never had a conscience about wenching before!'

James crossed the chamber and came face to face with him. 'I love her, Charles, and she is with child—my child. And what is more—I have already married her.'

The stunned silence in the King's bedchamber was so intense it was almost tangible. At length Charles spoke. 'How? And who is she?' There was no anger or reproach in his voice.

'Anne Hyde. We were contracted in Breda last November and married at Worcester House two weeks ago.'

'Edward Hyde's daughter,' mused Charles. 'And when is the child due to be born?'

'In three months,' replied James.

Charles looked thoughtfully into the fire for a time, then his eyes narrowed. 'I fear Chancellor Hyde is not going to be well pleased about this—I take it he is still in ignorance of his daughter's royal marriage?'

'Yes. No one knows of it but your chaplain, who married us, and Tom Butler.'

'I fancy Hyde will be in a towering rage when he discovers. I do not mind your alliance with Anne, for she is a virtuous, sensible maid, though not what one might call fair of face. It is Hyde's reaction I fear—such an upright, highly moral man is like to explode when he hears his daughter has been a royal bedfellow. And he knows his popularity is not of the highest. His enemies might well construe that he used his daughter to gain royal concessions, honours even.

'Ah James, you were right. Problems never come singly. But this one must be handled delicately. 'Twere best to break the news gently to Hyde myself.'

James poked his toe sullenly into the spaniel's flank. 'If it makes the position any better, I could possibly get out of the marriage,' he grunted. 'Charles Berkeley thinks I could claim the marriage was invalid because I did not have your consent. Moreover, he claims to have bedded Anne himself—and says he was not the only one.'

Charles bent to retrieve the spaniel from James' marauding foot. 'Charles Berkeley, as you well know, is a liar as well as a libertine. One has only to look at Anne Hyde to know her for a virtuous maid. If you have made her otherwise, then you do right to marry her. You like her, do you not?'

'Yes—well enough.'

'Then we'll leave matters as they are, and I shall send for Hyde to tell him,' concluded Charles firmly.

God, what a week this has been, he thought to himself when James had gone. One damn worry after another. Soon Mary would arrive—and she would have a great deal to say when she discovered her brother was married to her erstwhile maid of honour! And then his mother—what would Queen Henrietta say of her son's marriage to the child of a man she hated?

Charles sighed heavily. It was no use. Everywhere one looked there was nothing but problems and trouble. And there was no respite to be found anywhere, certainly not with Barbara, in the mood she was in at present. Oh for a loving, undemanding creature in whose arms he could forget for a while!

With this thought, a lovely, wide-eyed face flashed into his mind. A sweet maid with deep blonde hair and trusting brown eyes. He puzzled a moment. Ah yes! the pretty little foreign wench at the masked ball who had so inconveniently fainted, he remembered her now. Dainty she was, slender as a reed but with a body that held promise. She was just the kind of creature he needed. He rose quickly and summoned Progers.

'Lady Arabella Davenham's protégée, Sire,' Progers said in answer to his question. 'Fräulein Birke, I believe, Fräulein Topaz Birke.'

'And we did not enquire after her health, did, we, Progers? That was very remiss of us. I want you to rectify this at once.'

'But Sire, it is the middle of the night—growing near dawn,' Progers protested.

'First thing in the morning, then. And when you are satisfied she is well, bid her come to me in the evening.'

Progers bowed and withdrew. He had had this kind of confidential command entrusted to him on many occasions before, and knew exactly what was expected of him.

SEVENTEEN

TOPAZ had passed the last few days as in a dream, scarcely seeing or hearing what went on around her. And at night she escaped to the solitude of her own chamber.

She lay wide-eyed, staring at the tester above her, still waiting for the tears of disappointment and grief to overwhelm her, but none came. From time to time she heard a far-away clock strike the hours and a watchman's cries. Nothing stirred in her. No grief, no regret for the past, and no hope for the future either. Life lay like an arid desert, a long, blank emptiness stretching before and behind her.

From force of habit she found she was holding the well-fingered rosary beads in her hand, but for the first time she could remember, no spontaneous prayer to St. Teresa sprang to her lips. What was the use? St. Teresa had done all she had asked of her, had led her to Charles, but to what end? Charles was not only King of England and far out of her reach, but he had not even the faintest recollection of having met and made love to her. All this time she had been carrying her love for this man like a torch to illumine her darkest hours, and all the time it had been a self-deception.

Topaz groaned and stirred. Realization of the futility of her search clamped down on her heart with the heavy, cold grip of a vice. Outside she could hear the birds beginning their dawn chorus. Mechanically she rose and dressed, the leaden weight inside her slowing her movements and dulling her awareness, so that it was with a start of surprise that she turned and saw Sophie standing in the connecting doorway.

'I did not lock this door again, Topaz,' Sophie said softly, 'in case you should feel like talking, or simply in need of company.'

She waited, but Topaz made no reply. Vaguely her brain was registering the fact that Sophie was making overtures of friendship again and that she ought to acknowledge the gesture.

'Thank you, you are kind,' she said stiffly. Sophie came slowly into the chamber, still in her bedgown.

'Topaz, I do not wish to intrude upon your privacy, but it is obvious to me and to my mother that something has gone awry with you. It pains my mother to see you thus. If there is aught—aught, either of us can do for you, please do not hesitate to ask us.'

She waited again. It was a magnanimous effort on her part to be thus forthcoming, Topaz knew, and it could not be entirely Lady Arabella's persuasive tongue which had encouraged her to speak. Topaz turned slowly from the window.

'I am deeply grateful, Sophie, both to you and to your mother for your concern. But I assure you there is naught you nor she nor anyone can do.'

Sophie waited expectantly. Topaz went on, 'I know she must be very puzzled at this sudden change.'

'Indeed she is,' interrupted Sophie. 'A few days ago you were bright-eyed and eager for the ball, then suddenly you have an attack of the vapours and thereafter no one can talk with you, you are so—so strange, so withdrawn and dazed.'

'I know,' said Topaz. 'It was a sudden and unexpected shock that caused it.'

'Can you not tell me of it, Topaz?' asked Sophie. 'Talking may help.'

Topaz shook her head slowly. 'I doubt it will, but I feel I owe you some explanation in return for your kindness. You may remember, I was anxious to trace an old friend—a man —in London.'

'Ah, yes—Charles Barlow, was it not? I remember—and Jason told me he would try to help you. But why this attack? Topaz, did you see him again?'

'I did—at the ball.'

Sophie eyed her curiously, and Topaz thought she could see a gleam of understanding cross Sophie's face. 'You may have guessed—he was my lover, Sophie, a long time ago, in Germany.'

Sophie's face registered open surprise. 'So that was why you were so anxious to find him?' she said slowly. 'Did you hope to marry him?' When Topaz did not reply at once, Sophie went on, 'I fear you did, you are so ignorant and trusting. You do not know men as they really are—grasping and indifferent. If you had been more worldly-wise, you would not have been so foolhardy as to leave the safety of your home to follow him across Europe.'

Topaz smiled wryly. 'I had little choice in the matter,' she said. 'When my stepfather discovered I was with child by the Englishman, he would have put me into a nunnery.' Ignoring the startled look on Sophie's face she went on, 'I had either to do as he bade me, or go in search of my lover. I chose the latter.'

It was strange, she thought, I had no intention of talking about this to anyone, and here I am telling Sophie, of all people. Sophie, whom she had always regarded as standoffish and diffident, was annoyed and amazed in turn, as she listened eagerly to Topaz's tale of her adventures, culminating in her meeting with Lady Arabella after the birth of her dead child.

Sophie rose and paced up and down the chamber. 'I' faith, I have never heard of such inhumanity!' she raged. 'Men! A fickle fellow who would love you and leave you, and a cruel stepfather who would not help you! And what happened at the ball, Topaz?' She turned and faced Topaz, a kindly light in her eyes. 'Did he refuse to acknowledge your child? Would he not marry you?'

Topaz felt the cold numbness clawing inside her again. 'No,' she said stiffly, then dropped her gaze to the floor and added quietly, 'He knew me not.'

'What?' Sophie's voice snapped like a broken violin string. 'You mean—he did not recognize you?' Her tone registered absolute incredulity. Indeed, it seemed strange to her, too, thought Topaz, that a man should not recognize a woman he had seduced.

Sophie was fury personified. She paced angrily up and down again, pouring forth her scorn and vituperation on all men, and finally stopped before Topaz.

'Surely you will not let him off thus lightly,' she said, her eyes narrowed with determination. 'Surely you will tell him who you are and what has befallen you, and demand recompense in some form?'

Topaz crossed slowly to stand by the window. It was full daylight outside now. 'Well?' pursued Sophie, 'It is not just that you should have borne so much suffering while he escapes scot-free. He must pay for his wrongdoing. Demand from him what you will—marriage, or payment in some other form. But you must not let him escape the result of his thoughtless actions. Make him pay!'

Make him pay! Sophie's voice rang in Topaz's ears, but it made no sense to her. She continued to gaze vacantly out of the window. Sophie came close and took her by the arm.

'Topaz, my dear,' she said quietly, 'I do not mean to sound vindictive. In truth, it is out of sympathy for your suffering that I speak. It must have taken great strength and endurance to suffer all you have done, and my admiration for you knows no bounds. But it seems grossly unfair that this Charles Barlow should remain in blissful ignorance of what he has done. He has paid not one jot of suffering or atonement for all the harm he has occasioned, and it is only right that he should know. Perchance he may regret the harm done, and offer some atonement of his own accord, but he must know.'

Topaz listened dully. If the man had been but a merchant, Sophie would perchance be right, but Sophie did not know who he really was or she would not advocate such a course. She must tell her.

Topaz turned slowly. 'Sophie, I know you mean well and I am grateful. But there was yet another shock awaiting me at Whitehall. You see, not only did he not recognize me but I also discovered that Charles Barlow was in fact—Charles Stuart.'

Sophie dropped her hand to her side. Her eyes grew wide and her jaw gaped.

'Dear God—the King!'

Sophie was thunderstruck. For a few moments she stood as if paralysed, then her agile brain summed up the situation in the light of this new evidence. She sat on the edge of the bed.

'Marriage then is obviously out of the question,' she said purposely, 'but what I said still holds good. There is no reason why you should not demand recompense for your suffering, even from His Majesty.'

'I do not wish to avenge my wrongs,' said Topaz. 'I feel no bitterness, no hatred. In fact I can feel nothing.'

'It is not surprising,' commented Sophie drily. 'Such shocks would be enough to rob a lesser creature of her reason. But I am determined to see justice done if you will not. What swine men are! They think to indulge their animal instincts where they will, and then forget.'

'No, in truth, it was not like that!' Topaz protested. 'He loved me for the moment at least. Of that I am sure.'

Sophie looked at her pityingly. 'I would not hurt you for the world, Topaz, but you must know that Charles Stuart has loved many women for the moment, and to each of them he has been—generous, when requested. There are many now living on an annuity from him, some of them with his bastard children to support. Many now live in an elegance they would never have known but for His Majesty's generous acknowledgement of their—favours.'

She waited for this information to sink in. Topaz was watching her wide-eyed. Was it truly her Charles Sophie was describing? Her first reaction was to reject the repulsive notion, but then scraps of remembered conversation trickled back to her, gossip about the King and his past mistresses, and the current one, Barbara Palmer, who made continual demands on him.

For the first time since the ball, Topaz felt sensation returning to her. The numbness was gradually being replaced by a constriction in her throat and a tingling in her heart. Was it possible she had been taken in by a practised deceiver, a man of calculated charm and smoothness? Was it possible she had been kept alive by her love for a man to whom an idyll such as at Torwald was but a pastime? She felt nauseated at the thought. It was one of the bitterest moments of all, she thought, far worse than the agony of childbirth, to find one's trust had been misplaced.

Sophie was eyeing her silently. 'Well?' she demanded.

'I do not know what to do,' Topaz confessed. 'Perchance you are right, and he should know what has passed since he left me, but in any event, how could I see him?'

'That is soon dealt with. I can easily arrange for you to have a private audience with His Majesty, and the rest is up to you.'

'To what end, Sophie? What good can such a meeting possibly do?'

'As I have already told you, Charles Stuart is always mindful of his obligations—once he knows of them. You will be in a position to demand a house, servants, a carriage and a lifelong annuity at the least, and if you have a mind to it, a title would not be outside your reach.'

'Oh no!' Topaz's eyes widened in horror. 'I could not be so vengeful,' she cried.

'Vengeful? To make a man pay belatedly for his cruel maltreatment? You have lost your home and patrimony on his account, your virtue and your child. Is the memory of all this suffering so soon forgotten? Is it not good for a man to atone for his sins on this earth?'

Topaz felt the tingle growing into a smarting pain. At last the vacuum inside her, the dreadful emptiness and deadness, was being replaced by a new and powerful emotion. Sophie was right. How dared this man make use of her for his pleasure, as he had done countless others, and never know a moment's anguish for all the suffering he caused!

She faced the other girl squarely. 'You are right, Sophie. I shall see Charles and tell him all, and perchance he will make amends.'

'Not perchance. You must ensure that he does,' replied Sophie.

'Very well.'

'Good. Then that is settled. Let us go down now,' said Sophie, rising and crossing to the door. 'The others will be already at breakfast.' She opened the door, then turned again to Topaz. 'You will not change your mind and relent? You will seek an audience with His Majesty, will you not?'

Before Topaz could reply, a resonant voice interrupted.

'There is no need.' Jason was standing outside the door. Sophie stepped back to allow him to enter. He stood just inside the door and looked at Topaz solemnly. 'A page has just arrived from Sir Edward Progers, the King's valet, with a message for you, Topaz. He presents his service to you, and bids you attend at the Palace at eleven tonight.'

He delivered the message impassively, then added, 'The page is below, awaiting your answer.'

Sophie's startled look changed to one of triumph. 'There!' she said with satisfaction. 'A royal invitation! It could not be more opportune. Tell the page Mistress Birke will be pleased to attend.'

Jason turned his sombre face towards her. 'You know what this message implies?' he asked.

'Of course, His Majesty has a fancy to Topaz. And why not, pray? As it chances, it suits Topaz's ends to see him tonight, so please bid the page to take back his answer.'

Topaz listened to this interchange in silence, but inwardly her feelings churned. She was almost beginning to regret her promise to Sophie but it would seem that fate had placed a golden opportunity before her, as if to confirm that this was the right course of action. Resolutely she looked into Jason's puzzled, enquiring face. 'Pray do as Sophie says,' she said quietly but firmly. 'I will be pleased to accept the invitation.'

Jason wheeled about and strode from her chamber without a word. Topaz knew by his manner that he was angry and bewildered; perchance he would even believe she was truly a whore at heart after all, to accept what was undoubtedly an invitation into the royal bed. The thought saddened her, but maybe later, when she was no longer so confused, she could explain to him. . . .

As the day passed, Topaz felt more and more like a dead creature that had been revived. Where formerly there had been no aim in life, now she had a goal. Bless Sophie for her kindly concern—it was she who had wrought the change. Topaz felt firmly convinced now that a wretched, weak, vain man who used women wholesale and indiscriminately deserved no better than the treatment she was to give him. He would not escape scot-free; as Sophie had said, he must pay for his sins! Did he know the pain of bearing and losing a child? Did he know the misery of living in squalor and degradation, maligned and misunderstood? Not he! But by heaven, he would know what he had caused, and pay he would!

Topaz began to grow exultant as evening approached. Tonight's moment of triumph would help to atone for the last eighteen months. It was good to feel the blood coursing through her veins again. She was alive, and there was still fighting spirit in her, as he would discover.

As dusk was falling she went into the library. Before a roaring log fire a pair of velvet-clad legs stretched out towards the hearth. As she closed the door, Jason rose from his seat.

He was holding something in his hand. He looked at her uncomfortably for a moment, then said, 'I have something for you that I meant to give you on the night of the ball, but we were separated and the opportunity did not arise.'

He was standing stiffly before her. 'What is it?' Topaz asked.

'A bauble—a ring I saw in a shop and which I thought at the time appropriate for you.' He stretched out his palm. Topaz took the ring from his hand and looked closely at it in the firelight. A golden stone glittered on a heavy chased gold band.

'It is very pretty—thank you, Jason,' she said, and sat on the chair near the fire. She put the ring on her finger and twisted it admiringly. Jason sat down again.

'Do you still intend to go to the Palace tonight?' he asked gruffly.

Topaz sighed. Explanations now would be too lengthy. 'I must,' she said briefly, then added, 'What is this stone, Jason? I have not seen such a one before.'

'It is a topaz—your birthstone,' he answered drily, 'and

its significance was what made me consider it appropriate—until now.'

'Its significance?' repeated Topaz. 'Tell me, Jason—what does a topaz signify?'

He looked at her curiously a moment before replying. 'Fidelity,' he answered curtly.

His abrupt tone made Topaz realize that his opinion of her had indeed lessened as a result of her accepting the King's invitation. It was ironic, she thought with a bitter smile. Here was Jason practically accusing her of fickleness, yet if the truth were known, fidelity had been her watchword for the last eighteen months.

For a year and a half she had been faithful to the constant memory and unswerving love of a man who had never known and would never know, the meaning of the word. What a stupid, blind dupe she had been! But there would be no more suffering in silence. Tonight she would speak her mind, not to Jason, but to Charles Stuart.

'I am very grateful to you, Jason, but I cannot accept it,' she said, giving the ring back to him. Then she rose and went to her chamber to prepare.

EIGHTEEN

SOPHIE accompanied Topaz to the vestibule. She ran an approving eye over her cinnamon velvet gown, lowcut, and overlaced with a busk bodice that pushed her breasts high. She had been most adamant that Topaz looked her most beautiful—'Charles appreciates a beauty,' she had said, 'and it were best if you are to gain what you desire.'

She helped Topaz into her fur-lined cloak. 'Now remember, Topaz, you are not to relent when you see a soft light in his eyes—men were arch-deceivers ever. Hold fast to your purpose.'

'I will, never fear,' replied Topaz quietly. The bell at the gate rang loudly and a porter entered.

'Sir Richard Conyers, ma'am, presents his compliments,' he said. Topaz saw the eager light that leapt into Sophie's eyes. 'So late?' Sophie asked.

'His horse has cast a shoe, ma'am, and is lame. He stopped to ask for help.'

'Bid him enter, Hackett,' she said, 'and then conduct Mistress Birke to Whitehall. The ostler will see to the horse.'

Hackett turned and went. Sophie squeezed Topaz's arm. 'Go now—and God speed.'

As Topaz crossed the yard to where the coach stood waiting, she saw the tall, greying, distinguished-looking man who handed his horse over to the ostler and climbed the flight of stone steps to the house. Sophie stood framed in the torchlight at the door, a welcoming smile on her face.

Perhaps Sophie had found the kind of man she sought at

last, thought Topaz. Strange, her relationship begins as mine with Charles ends. Life is strange—growth, flux, change and decay. Nothing is constant. There lies the misery of it—nothing is constant.

The coach jolted and jerked through the night along the cobbled streets, westward again towards Westminster. How different from last time I came this way, she thought, my heart high with hope. This time I come full of purpose and steel-hard determination to exact payment. That shallow, fickle creature she had misguidedly loved so long would know the extent of his thoughtlessness this night. Heaven help him, but she would spare him not one detail of the suffering he had caused!

The coach clattered to a halt, and a liveried servant led her through winding passageways and into a large chamber, where he left her. Topaz looked about her.

In a huge fireplace surmounted by a vast carved overmantel a cheerful seacoal fire was crackling restlessly. High plaster walls were decorated with gilded coats of arms, and a bracket clock on the wall ticked slowly and relentlessly. The high windows were screened by heavy velvet drapes reaching down to the parquet floors and up to the elaborate strapwork ceiling. The high-backed chairs and long oak table with squat bulbous legs gave the room a heavy, deliberate air—a room for momentous decisions, and earnest debate. Charles no doubt conferred with his ministers in this chamber. Tonight perhaps it would be the scene for another momentous event, Topaz thought, when Charles would be brought face to face with his own actions.

She composed herself in a chair by the fire to wait.

Charles sent Chiffinch from the room as soon as the valet had disrobed him. He addressed Progers.

'She is here now?'

'Yes Sire. I have put her to wait in one chamber and Mistress Palmer in another. I fear Mistress Palmer is somewhat impatient, though, Sire.'

Charles grunted. 'As ever,' he commented. 'What means she by coming here now, after refusing so many days to spite me? Ah well, keep the little one amused, Progers, while I talk to Barbara. Show her my trinkets, if you will, and then bring Mistress Palmer in.'

Damn the woman for her impertinence! he thought. She thinks she can come and go as she pleases, as though she were the sovereign, not I. And tonight I had a strong fancy for a gentle, blissful interlude—with Barbara it was never gentle. The situation was like to be explosive either way—whether she were in a mood for love or gain. Never mind, after she had gone he could unwind with the little one.

He sighed and leaned back in his chair to await the storm. . . .

Topaz sat forward quickly, her heart leaping in expectation as the heavy door swung open, but it was not Charles who entered. It was the tall gentleman she remembered from the Stone Gallery.

'I regret His Majesty has been detained by other pressing business, mistress,' he said gravely, 'but he would be obliged if you would be patient and wait a little.'

'Gladly,' said Topaz. 'I am in no hurry.'

'Then if you would follow me, ma'am, I will lead you to His Majesty's closet where his collection of valuable *objets d'art* are stored.'

As Topaz rose to follow him, he added. 'Few are granted the privilege of entering this closet, ma'am. You are honoured.' And he turned and led the way.

Alone in the large chamber Topaz gazed around her at the magnificent paintings adorning the walls. Holbein, Danckerts,

Verelst, Van Dyck she read on the frames, but her mind was elsewhere, and not on the familiarity of the serene Dutch faces among the portraits. She wandered restlessly among the cabinets displaying the most intricate needlework samplers and delicate miniatures, sparkling jewels and ivory statues, maps and charts, and among ornate clocks and timepieces, but the beauty of these treasures did not penetrate her consciousness.

So much Charles owned! Sophie was right. Recompense to a former mistress would not hit him too hard. He could afford it. She picked up a magnificent ruby, lying couched in a nest of velvet. This and many more like it she could demand and no doubt obtain—and it would leave scarcely an imprint on his memory or his coffers.

But of what use to her were rubies? It was his love she had come to this country to seek, and now it was impossible. What then did she really hope to gain from this meeting?

Again Sophie's words flashed into her mind. He must pay! Perhaps it would at least teach him to think before treating other poor souls so lightly. She drew herself upright. Yes, she must reproach him, no matter how distasteful the meeting would be.

Carefully she rehearsed her speech. She must be word-perfect when they met, lest his charm should throw her off-balance.

Topaz was sick with disillusion. After this night what was there left to do, but to abandon all hope and return whence she came? But the thought of returning to Torwald offered no hope for the future either. Never again would she hold out hopes for the future, but take each day as it came.

Gloomily she walked to the door. What was occupying Charles so long? She was anxious to have done with this business and be away. She opened the door and looked out, but the passageway was deserted.

Thinks he to put me in more submissive mood by keeping

me waiting? she thought angrily. I'll not be kept dancing attendance here like some little strumpet anxious for a gold coin or two! She closed the door after her and set off along the passage. Numerous doors opened off, and Topaz hesitated which way to go. Through the arched doorway at the end, she encountered yet another long corridor receding into the distance.

Suddenly she heard voices, followed by the sound of a heavy door slamming. Not wishing to be caught hanging about furtively like a spy, she hurried through the nearest door and found herself in a small ante-chamber. She closed the door behind her and leaned against it, her heart pounding. Timid mouse, she reproached herself, you who came here full of determination to reproach a king!

Outside in the corridor she heard the swish of taffeta skirts and giggles as a low voice murmured. The footsteps passed, then stopped further down the passage. Unable to go out the way she came, Topaz crossed to the other door in the chamber, and as she approached it her steps were suddenly arrested by a high-pitched woman's voice on the other side.

'I could not have come,' the voice cried. 'I had the most ghastly megrim!'

'Indeed?' a low voice replied, and Topaz's heart leapt. One word—but she recognized at once the vibrant, velvet timbre. It was Charles—with a woman. Topaz seethed with anger.

'Indeed?' said Charles, eyeing the tall, graceful figure pacing restlessly before him. She was beautiful, her emerald gown showing off to advantage the creamy texture of her skin. 'It is odd how opportunely you have attacks of the headache, Barbara, when it is convenient for you. Are you sure you did not refuse to come out of pique?'

The pacing stopped. Barbara flung herself impetuously at his knees as he reclined in his chair. 'Beloved, do you really think I would refuse to come to you when you want me? You know that every minute I spend away from you is agony! It is true I was disappointed that you did not see fit to grant me what I asked, but—pique? Never!' She caressed his arm through the fine linen of his shirt.

Charles smiled disbelievingly. He knew Barbara's ability to play-act. She knew she could wriggle out of any uncomfortable situation by applying her feminine appeal, and he was well aware that that was what she was doing. When he did not answer immediately she took his hand gently, her head resting on his knee, and guided the long, thin fingers into her bodice, thrusting her breasts to meet them.

Charles needed no second invitation. He curled his fingers tightly about her till she winced and looked up at him in delight. With his free hand he loosened her bodice and drew it down to her waist, exposing her full, high breasts.

'Charles, my love,' she murmured ecstatically as her hand slid up his thigh, 'Will you not reconsider? A title for Roger—and thus for me—in view of my father's loyalty to the Royalist cause, if for nothing else?'

He stiffened and let her go. So that was it! She was still after that damned title! Barbara saw her mistake and tried to rectify it.

'But no more of that now—come, my love.' She stood up and tried to draw him towards the huge bed, but Charles resisted. He knew full well that she would utter much the same words again at the height of their ecstasy—dammit, why should she always spoil their happiness with these unending demands?

The huge, round violet eyes were watching him reproachfully. Charles reached up and ran his fingers through the long, thick red hair. 'I am tired, my pet. Not now,' he said, and saw at once the huge round eyes narrow and start to flash.

'Tired?' she snapped. 'Of what? Of me? Has some other strumpet taken your fancy, is that it?'

'Od's fish, no. 'Tis a surfeit of state matters that have eaten up my energy, my love, I assure you. Why, only today I feared Chancellor Hyde would have a sudden apoplexy, the way he raged. It was all James and I could do to control him.'

'Over what did he rage?' The blue eyes were gazing at him in interest. She knelt by his knee again, and Charles relaxed. Once Barbara forgot her demands and talked reasonably, she had a lively, intelligent mind he found he could converse with easily and satisfyingly.

'Poor man, I had to disclose to him that his daughter, Anne, was secretly married to my brother James, and moreover, is with child by him,' he told her. Her eyes widened as she digested the information, then she chuckled maliciously. She had no love for Hyde, for he openly showed his disapproval of her position as the King's mistress. She was enjoying the thought of the anger and dismay he must have felt over his daughter.

'What did he say?' she asked eventually.

'Well, when we managed to get any sense out of him—he was purple most of the time—he said he would prefer his daughter to be the Duke's whore rather than his wife, and he would prefer to see her in a dungeon in the Tower, beheaded even. He was near out of his mind, poor fellow. We could make no progress with him. He finally went off home to confine Anne to her chamber to keep her out of James' reach. But it is not over yet, I fear. We shall have more trouble from that quarter unless I am much mistaken.'

Barbara turned the scene over in her mind, then turned to Charles. 'And this has sapped your energy?' she asked.

'This—and the many other problems I have had to face of late—Minette's marriage—Mary and my mother coming—Harry's death—and soon the regicides will have to be hanged.

Parliament is bent on revenge, though I would it were all done with. So many worries. . . .'

'Then you are in need of relaxation more often, my love,' Barbara pronounced. 'I could help you forget, if you would let me. Why do you restrict my coming hither to only four nights in the week? I die a thousand deaths without you the other three nights. My body needs you, Charles,' she said, her eyes large and pleading again, 'and you need mine.'

Charles smiled. 'You have Roger—cannot your husband content your greedy body on the nights we are separated?' he said laughingly.

'Roger!' Barbara's voice was thick with scorn, and her eyes savage as she sat upright. 'He has a prick no bigger than my little finger—he could not even satisfy a cat! Not like you, my love,' she added, her snarl changing to a purr as she slid her fingers smoothly along his thigh.

Charles sighed. He was emphatically not of a mood tonight for the frenetic cavorting that lovemaking with Barbara invariably involved. He was a fool, he thought, deliberately to forgo the opportunity of mounting such a willing steed, one that would be ridden tirelessly again and again throughout the night, but he truly did not have the stomach for it this night. He brushed her hand away.

Undaunted she slid her lovely arms about his shoulders, so that her glossy hair hung across his face, soft and sweetly-scented. 'About the title . . .' she began in a wheedling tone.

'Enough!' Charles sat upright. 'I will hear no more of a title,' he said firmly.

Barbara's mood changed instantly. 'Ungrateful beast!' she yelled, standing to her full height, her eyes flashing angrily. 'You take all I have to offer you, but will listen to no requests in return! A strumpet from the streets, filthy and full of the pox, would gain more from you than I!' Then, seeing her words had no effect, Barbara tried another tack.

'My love,' she cooed, 'You know there is naught I would not do for you, do you not? A title is a small thing to ask in return.' Charles looked into the dark eyes, moist with unshed tears. He was not deluded. He knew from past experience that she could turn on her tears as easily as any accomplished actress, and that she frequently did so, since he had once described her tearful eyes as drowned violets, for she felt that she could sway him thus.

'No more, Barbara, I am weary,' he said, 'I can take no more. I am overwhelmed by the cares of state, and would have a brief respite. . . .'

'A pox on you and your respite!' she screamed—just like any fishwife, he reflected wearily, and bore in silence the stream of abuse she heaped upon him. At the height of her raging she seized a small statue from the mantelshelf and hurled it across the chamber, where it crashed against the panelling and fell, shattered, to the floor. Then she turned and advanced upon him, her eyes glittering. The firelight glistened on her naked breasts, and Charles thought that on any other occasion the sight would have driven him mad with desire for her. But not tonight.

'There is one thing more you should know, Sire, before you finally decline my modest enough request,' she hissed malevolently. 'It would seem I am with child!'

Charles raised his eyebrows. 'Are you sure?'

She shrugged petulantly. ' 'Tis like enough. It must be some several weeks since I last had the flux. So there, my love,' she said insolently, her hands on her hips, 'is a very good reason why I should bear a title ere I bear a child.'

'I do not follow your reasoning, Barbara.'

She raised her hands in a despairing gesture, then slapped them to her sides impatiently. 'Blockhead! Would you have your son born a commoner, and a bastard to boot?'

Charles eyed her calmly. 'Are you so sure it would be my

child?' he asked equably. 'From all I hear, you vent your rutting instincts liberally enough with others beside myself.'

The look Barbara turned on him contained enough vitriol to annihilate an army. Slowly her mouth fell open, but she remained silent for the moment. Then she raised one arm. 'I swear, by all that's holy,' she said in a low voice, 'that if you do not acknowledge the child and grant me my title, I shall murder the bastard here, in the Palace, before all your Court.'

He knew she was capable of it. He rose from his chair and put an arm about her. 'Come now, there is naught to be gained by hysterical outbursts,' he said consolingly, his mouth against her hair. 'Let us talk of it tomorrow. Do you go home now and sleep.'

She snuggled close to his chest. 'I would rather sleep with you, Charles,' she murmured, reaching for the fastening on his breeches. God, but her body was warm and inviting, supple and curving in to his own. He held her at arm's length.

'Good night, Barbara,' he said.

'Have done with you then,' she snapped as she let him go. 'I'll not beg your favours. I'll find another to satisfy my wants this night.' She pulled up her bodice and fastened it angrily.

'Do that,' Charles murmured agreeably. 'I shall see you tomorrow.'

'We shall see!' she snapped, then added in a quieter tone, 'Mayhap you will have news for me of a title?'

'For pity's sake—no more,' said Charles. 'Begone.'

She snatched up her velvet cloak and slammed out. Charles sank down on the edge of the bed in relief. Thank God! Perhaps now he could sleep.

The door opened and a bewildered Progers entered. 'The lady near knocked me flying when I asked her if I should call her coach, she swept by in such a towering rage,' he said.

'I know, Progers. And now I will sleep.'

'But Your Majesty. . . .'

'What is it, man?'

'The young lady, Sire, Fräulein Birke. . . .'

'Od's fish! I had completely forgot! Is she still waiting, Progers?'

'I left her in your closet, admiring your treasures, Sire.'

'Poor child, to wait so long, forgotten. Fetch her to me, and then get yourself off to bed. I shall want no more till morning.'

Progers went. Charles stretched and yawned. The fulfilment of the day he had been looking forward to for so long had been driven from his mind by Barbara's importunate visit, and it was comforting to find one still had something pleasurable to anticipate. For a long time now he had been faithful to Barbara—her savage, greedy, sensual intoxication had been manna to him—but now it was time to relax. After all, she had Roger—and Chesterfield—and others of a lowlier station, it was rumoured, to satisfy her. . . .

NINETEEN

AT the first words she had overheard, Topaz had been seized with an almost uncontrollable anger, that this man who had so cruelly deceived her was still playing his wanton games with yet another poor wretch, on the very night he had invited *her* to come to him. Was the man an insatiable monster? Her first impulse had been to wrench open the door that separated them and give him the full measure of her rage.

She had hesitated a moment, stunned by the force of her own anger, and then realized when she heard the name Barbara that this was the Mistress Palmer of whom all London was talking, the woman Charles was so enamoured with. But Barbara's words had shown little love for Charles, only greed for herself. Poor Charles, if he received only love of this kind.

Topaz could only guess at what went on in the chamber during the lulls in their intermittent conversation, but it needed little imagination to conclude that Charles was far from happy with this creature. During the one occasion she had ceased her demands to listen to him, Charles had made it clear that he was a very worried and unhappy man, but within moments she had resumed her insistent demands, mindless of his sadness. He had mentioned but briefly the multitude of complexities piling up on him, and the sudden death of his brother had obviously taken him unawares. And now that creature was possibly carrying his child, as she had done. But Barbara would make sure she gained from her unwanted pregnancy.

Poor Charles, Topaz reflected. Her anger was dissipated as

quickly as it had been born. He was still the vain, feckless man she had come to reproach, but now she could see also that he was weak, insecure, and very unsure of the love of any man. She remembered what she had heard from a fervently royalist Lady Arabella about his father's death, his mother, loving but undemonstrative; she remembered how his family had always been separated in exile, and Lady Arabella's stories of how the child Charles always took a piece of wood to bed with him stubbornly, to comfort him in the dark. Father murdered, brother dead—the Stuart family was indeed cursed, it would seem. No wonder Charles suffered from insecurity.

Now she understood. The stories of Charles and his numerous women—he was seeking love wherever he could in order to reassure himself that he was loved. In times of stress he sought a woman as a babe seeks its mother. Every woman was another billet of wood, to console and strengthen him in his need. And now, more than ever before, with so much worry, Charles needed love.

The emptiness left by receding anger was quickly filled by pity. To think she had come thus far in order to make him suffer, and all the time he was suffering in a way few could understand. Pointless now was the interview Sophie had planned, but she would understand when Topaz explained why she had come away from Whitehall without seeking recompense. . . .

She turned and tiptoed from the little chamber. The corridor was deserted as she retraced her steps towards the closet, but as she neared the door an agitated Progers hurried into view.

'Mistress Birke! I have been seeking you everywhere,' he said reproachfully. 'Come, His Majesty awaits you,' and he turned quickly. Topaz had no course but to follow him.

He led her into a vast, firelit chamber, murmured her name and withdrew. Topaz walked to the centre of the room before she saw the limp figure, its forehead leaning against the glass of the window. He straightened quickly and came to meet her. By the light of the fire Topaz could see his face and she heard the sound of her own quick, indrawn breath.

Charles was smiling, but it was a tired, haggard smile. There was no welcoming light in the dark, slumbrous eyes, and she could see fine lines etched about his eyes that were not there in Torwald. He wore no wig, and his tall frame seemed thinner and frailer, clad as he was only in breeches and a full-sleeved white shirt. No king this, but a tired, disillusioned man.

Topaz felt her heart quicken in sympathy for him. A few silver hairs were interlaced with the black at his temples. He was prematurely ageing from the stress of all his cares. Poor Charles. . . .

Charles welcomed the coolness of the windowpane against his hot, aching head. God, he felt so old and tired! Only thirty years of age, but he felt like a man of sixty! On top of everything else, Barbara was trying to hold him to ransom over her bastard, but she could be lying. He knew her—she was capable of stooping to any level to get what she wanted.

He heard Progers enter and announce the girl and made a determined effort. He must be chivalrous at all costs, and went to meet her with a deliberate smile.

What a pretty little thing she was in the firelight, her hood thrown back and her glorious gold hair piled high. The amber eyes watched him soberly as he unlaced her cloak and drew it from her. Yes, the figure was as he remembered it—fine and dainty, virginal almost in contrast to Barbara's full-blown, voluptuous form. Her firm little breasts were constrained too high and tight in that horrible bodice thing she was wearing—he must take that from her as soon as possible.

He allowed himself a moment's indulgence as he visualized

removing all her other garments, and sinking his tired head between those white little maiden breasts. . . .

'Forgive me, Mistress Topaz, for keeping you waiting,' he murmured, wondering whether it was too early to reach up and unpin that glorious hair. She looked so fragile and ethereal—she might yet be a virgin and would not welcome too hasty advances.

'It matters not, Sire,' she replied quietly. Her voice was low and husky, so far removed from Barbara's shrill, piercing demands. An angel, that was what she was, an angel of mercy, come to comfort him in his hour of need. But gently, Charles, he reminded himself. He wanted her all soft, yielding compliance, not a stiff, white little virginal body lying beside him in mute anger, outraged and cold.

He led her to the fireside. Her hand seemed so small and defenceless in his, her fingers fluttering slightly like some poor hapless fledgling fallen from its nest. Charles loved small, helpless animals, and he was touched by her. Moreover, there was something indefinably familiar about her, though he could not place what it was. Perchance it was the resemblance to the little sister Minette he had not seen for so long. She, too, had the same innocent, vulnerable air about her as a child. Poor Minette—he fancied she did not realize what she was undertaking in wanting to be contracted to that strange, malevolent brother of Louis.

Poor Minette. She would be deeply distressed by young Harry's death, for she was closer to him than any of them. She had been convinced he held more promise than either of his brothers, and that bright spark of promise had been cut off so cruelly. . . .

He dragged his mind quickly back to the moment. The poor child standing quietly, her hand in his, was still watching him wide-eyed and silent. What was her name? Topaz—yes, that was it.

'Tell me, Topaz, where do you come from?' he asked her gently.

'From a little town in north Germany, near the Dutch border,' she replied. Strange, he thought. He had spent much of his exile amongst the Germans and Dutch, and their women were almost invariably large-boned and heavy-hipped and dull of countenance. He remembered how he had once dismissed them all as 'foggy', but not this little creature.

'Topaz, you are like a gentle ray of sunshine, come to illumine my dark hours,' he said earnestly, and was happy to see the warmth begin to glow in her eyes. 'Yes, sunshine in your eyes and in your beautiful hair,' he went on, raising a hand to loosen the comb. At once the pile of hair fell, thick and heavy, over her shoulders, the firelight picking out the gold so that it shone about her like a halo. Her lips began to curve into a smile. Good, she was beginning to mellow.

He took her hand and drew her down on the fur rug before the fire. Phoebe, his favourite spaniel, looked up reproachfully as he moved her gently aside with his toe, then crawled away under the bed to sleep undisturbed.

'Poor Phoebe!' he laughed softly. 'She is to litter soon and I am loth to disturb her rest, but my need of the rug is greater than hers at the moment. She shall have all the comfort she needs when her time comes.'

He looked soberly at the girl to see her reaction. She was smiling. He had not meant to show his concern for his dogs in order to impress her, but it was evident that she appreciated it. She laid her hand timidly on his sleeve.

'Methinks Your Majesty appears somewhat tired,' she said. Oh, what a lovely, low voice, melting and liquid as honey! 'Perchance you would prefer to sleep rather than to talk.'

He eyed her quizzically. No, he decided, it was not an invitation to bed. If Barbara had uttered them, such words would have been a direct invitation, but this child was so innocent, she meant no more than she said.

That busk she was wearing looked damnably uncomfortable! He laid his hand on her breast to loosen it, and saw the eyelids flutter as her fingers chased his, held them for a moment, then slowly let go. She was watching him, wide-eyed, and with her soft, curving lips gently parted, as he loosened the barrier busk and laid it aside, then returned to the pleasant task of unfastening her bodice. She did not help him, nor did she make any effort to stop him.

Aha! This was progress! A little gentle play for a time, and the bird was surely his!

From the moment Topaz laid eyes on his careworn face, all intention of making the carefully-rehearsed speech she had carried in her mind all day, died away completely. Oh Charles! My dear, beloved Charles! How you have aged and lost your sparkle! she cried inwardly, and her heart was pained to see him thus. If she had ever doubted it, she knew at this moment for certain that she still loved this man, king or commoner, happy or careworn and that she could never do anything to hurt him more than he had already been hurt.

She had still retained a glimmer of hope that when he touched her perhaps yet he would remember Torwald, but memory was not stirred, and she could not help the ache that returned to torment her. At his touch her hands had inadvertently flown to restrain him, but then sympathy for his sadness overflowed, and she stayed him not. . . . If I can do this much to alleviate your suffering, my darling, it is but a small thing I can do.

The warmth of the fire suffused her body as his long, thin hands caressed her gently. She remembered all too vividly the sensations he aroused in her once before, and was doing now again, and she relaxed and leaned against him. He evidently sensed her capitulation, for his hands moved more urgently, more seekingly, and he murmured soft words in her ear, words she had heard from his lips before.

'Topaz, Topaz my love,' he said in a husky voice, and she was content that he was so. Then suddenly he rose, drew her up by the hand, and swung her off her feet and carried her to the vast bed. Within moments he was lying close to her, his body hard-skinned and lean, and he caressed her face with his fingertips. Suddenly he stopped and looked at her curiously.

'I remember now, at the ball you said we had met before,' he said. 'I regret I am churl enough to forget the occasion—when was it, Topaz, and where?'

Topaz hesitated. Her heart was fluttering wildly after all those stroking caresses. Should she tell him, or let him take her for a maid merely anxious to please a king? Innate honesty prevailed.

' 'Twas a year and a half ago—in Germany—in a place called Torwald. You spent some time there with me, you and your friend, James Butler. But I knew you as Charles Barlow then.'

She watched the wonderment on his face change slowly as recollection returned, and he smiled in pleasure. 'Indeed, I remember now! Oh Topaz, how could I have forgotten your kindness to a poor, woebegone traveller? What an oaf you must think me!'

Topaz smiled and shook her head. ' 'Tis small wonder you forgot, Sire, with so many cares on your mind, and so much that has happened since.'

Instantly she regretted reminding him of his cares. The smile of pleasure faded from his face, and the dark eyes became sombre. He cradled her close in his arms.

'Ah, Topaz, how little I knew! I thought then that to be restored to my throne would mean the end of all poverty and unhappiness, and that thenceforward England would be a land of immeasurable peace and contentment. Yet in a few brief months—all this. . . .'

He buried his face in her hair a moment, then looked earnestly into her eyes.

'What brought you here, Topaz, hither to England? So far away from your secluded little Torwald?' The look was so dark, so intense and piercing that she felt all her love for him washing over her again, strong and undeniable as breakers on the seashore. Again she hesitated. Here was the cue Sophie would have asked for, the invitation to tell Charles the reason for her being here. The misery, the degradation, the death of his child—now was the opportunity to tell him all and watch the remorse grow in his smouldering eyes. But to hurt him further now would be like kicking one of those adoring spaniels he cherished. Topaz resolved that no matter how Sophie would rail, Charles should never know what she had undergone on his account.

'A dream, Sire,' she answered him. 'There was nothing for me in Torwald any more, so I came in search of a dream.'

A hint of a bitter smile crossed his lips. 'As do we all, little one. We all seek a dream. But I hope you find your contentment more easily than I mine. I fear we are accursed, we Stuarts. . . .' His heavy-lidded eyes were boring into her. 'Topaz,' he murmured, 'You were an angel of mercy to me once. Your kindness and gentleness sustained me when my fortunes were at a very low ebb. Can you find it in your heart to forgive me and show me that kindness again?'

For a moment Topaz rebelled. By kindness he meant giving herself to him, that much she knew now, but last time he had taken advantage of her ignorance. Now she knew of his many amorous adventures with women, was she to be but one more, just a moment's fancy yet again? She felt herself stiffen in his arms, but when she saw again the care and fatigue etched all over his dark, handsome face, she felt herself relenting.

Poor, poor Charles. Moreover, his gently moving hands were very persuasive. He was almost pathetic in his desperate desire for comfort.

Her love for him rose fiercely and protectively to the surface again. Oh my love, if no one else can render you this service tonight, then I can and will, she cried inwardly, and drew his head down on her bosom. He lay there, murmuring contentedly, and Topaz felt like a mother who has found again the child she had lost. She stroked and soothed him, uttering gentle words of comfort and reassurance, and gradually the hands ceased moving and the head lay heavy on her breast. His breathing grew slower and deeper, and Topaz lay stiff and cramped, not daring to move lest he was sleeping.

Finally, assured he was deeply asleep, she reached one arm out slowly and drew a silken coverlet over both their bodies. So great was her discomfort that she could not sleep, but took comfort from the fact that her beloved Charles lay content and at rest in her arms. This was what she had dreamt of so often, and now it was reality.

She felt his crisp hair curling under her chin. Poor Charles, so tired and misunderstood! At this moment he lay, so vulnerable and human, no king but a mere man. She longed to be able to comfort and cherish him always, to soothe away his cares and give him rest. But she was only too well aware of the gulf that separated them, the differences of nationality and religion, and the crown that rested on his noble, handsome head. Charles was a man of destiny. The crown he had yearned for carried with it authority and responsibility; never would he be in a position to act as he pleased. Poor Charles, simply a pawn in a political game that drained his strength. . . .

He stirred and turned over. In his sleep his hand stroked her body, and gradually he awoke. This time he knew her. 'Topaz, my love,' he breathed into her ear.

This time she knew exactly what he was about. So gentle

and loving were his actions that Topaz felt awakened in her sensations she had never known, and she climbed to a height of ecstasy she had never dreamed possible. Afterwards he slept, but Topaz lay all night and remembered the glory of the ecstasy.

Charles, my beloved, I shall love you all my life, she whispered, and fervently blessed St. Teresa for this night of supreme happiness at last, when she was able to give Charles the love and comfort he so desperately needed. . . .

TWENTY

CHARLES stretched leisurely and yawned. I' faith, he felt vastly refreshed this morning! He reached out an inquisitive arm, but the bed beside him was empty. He opened his eyes. Ah yes, Barbara was still in a fit of the sulks over that blasted title.

Suddenly he recollected the little maid—Topaz—he remembered now. He had borne her light little body to the bed when he had deemed the moment ripe, then—what? He must have fallen asleep from sheer exhaustion. He dimly remembered waking again—and yes, that time he had taken her. He could still sense the tight little body affording him infinite pleasure. Where the devil was she now?

He drew aside the bed curtains and swung his legs off the high bed. In the pale grey light of dawn he saw her, already dressed, standing at one of the windows, whose heavy drapes had been drawn back. The fire had died in the hearth, and the chamber was chill and grey.

'Topaz,' he said, climbing into his breeches and pulling on his shirt, 'You are abroad early.' In fact he thought it was late. He preferred his visitors by the backstairs to be gone long before dawn, but God! He had been so exhausted he had slept on and on. . . .

She did not move. She stood looking out, her huge brown eyes far away and thoughtful. In the pale half-light he could see clearly her fair young face with its finely-cut features, her soft hair and the firm young chin. So motionless, she looked like one of his marble statues, he thought. Or like Minette—with that air of trusting innocence. Dear girl!

He felt immensely grateful to this uncommonly naïve little creature; she had given him the moment of rest he had so earnestly sought. Perchance, if he treated her gently, she would agree to come again when Barbara became too taxing. She had none of Barbara's fire, but she was so relaxing by contrast; a mouse, but still, he was reluctant to let Progers take her away. . . . He came close to her and put his finger gently under her chin.

Topaz started from her reverie. She had not heard him wake or speak. She watched the slow smile curling the corners of his full lips, and felt content that she had helped to restore him in some measure.

'What are you watching so intently, little one?' he asked. 'There is naught out there but the river.' She watched him as he surveyed the view, the slow wreaths of clammy mist curling over the grey river, and the trees like skeletons, almost denuded of their leaves. He was still pale and care-lined, but the utterly drained and defeated look of last night was gone.

'The leaves are falling fast,' he commented absently. 'Life is all too brief. Soon the regicides must fall to the executioner just as surely as those leaves.' He was speaking more to himself than to her, a far-away look in his eyes. So soon again he was becoming absorbed in the cares of government. She shivered involuntarily. His mention of death suddenly recalled to her mind the omen of the chicken in the market place, the omen that was to change the whole course of her life. . . .

'You're shivering, child,' Charles said, putting an arm about her. 'I shall order wine and food for you, and a fire to warm you before you leave. Progers!'

'Thank you, I am neither hungry nor cold,' Topaz replied, 'but it is time I departed.'

'You will come to me again, Topaz?' he said eagerly, and

Topaz revelled in the warmth in his black eyes. She shook her head sadly.

'No, Sire,' she said. More than anything in the world she would prefer to be at this man's side, always, but she could see all too clearly the yawning chasm that separated their worlds.

A discreet knock at the door heralded Progers' entrance. He stood silent while Charles helped Topaz don her cloak.

'Perchance you will change your mind and come to me in my need again?' Charles whispered. 'You will be near enough to Whitehall.'

'No Sire, I think mayhap I shall return soon to Torwald, since my stepfather is now dead.'

He was standing by the door with her, holding her hands tightly in his. Progers' gaze was discreetly averted. Charles ran his fingertips lightly down her cheek. 'You are beautiful, Topaz,' he said. 'Beautiful and kind—a veritable saint. I shall remember you with love always.'

Topaz took one last look at the man she knew she would always love, the father of a child he never knew. 'Adieu,' she said quickly, then turned abruptly away, hastening out before Progers could lead the way.

Blindly she hurried along corridors and passageways, tears scalding her eyelids. Then she heard Progers' feet tap-tapping along behind her, anxious to overtake her, and slowed her steps.

He hastened anxiously to her side. 'His Majesty bade me give you this token,' he said breathlessly, proffering a velvet pouch. Topaz heard the tinkle of gold coins, and judged by the size of the pouch it must contain a vast sum. She pushed his hand away, and moved on. 'Allow me then, mistress, to order a coach for you,' Progers added, and Topaz nodded dumbly.

At the outer gate the chill damp October air enveloped

her, and Progers disappeared from view. Never again shall I enter Whitehall, she thought sadly. Never again shall I see my beloved. . . . She refused to allow the tears to come again, but jutted her chin defiantly. I have done all I can for him, and now I must make what I can of life without him, she thought resolutely—but oh! how bleak was the prospect!

Rain was falling fast now, and Topaz heard footsteps clatter on the cobblestones under the arched gateway. Progers and the coachman, she thought, but no one called her. Then she made out the shrouded figure of a man hunched in a cloak, standing under the arch. He turned slowly. She saw the plume in his hat hanging limp under the weight of mist and rain, and then the fair head as he doffed his hat and came towards her.

It was Jason. He came close and scanned her face, his blue eyes serious and anxious. Moist droplets clung to the blond hair.

'Topaz?' he said quietly. 'Are you well?'

She nodded. She could not understand why he was here when he had been so patently disapproving of her visit to Whitehall, and judging by the drenched look of him, he must have been waiting for some time. He seemed to read her surprise.

'Sophie told me all,' he said simply, and drew her arm through his. So that was it. Topaz sighed. Perchance she was leaving behind her for ever the love of her life, but it was comforting to be going into the arms of a family who cared about her. Dear Lady Arabella, so warm and motherly, and Sophie, whose kindly feelings had simply been concealed for a time beneath an intellectual shell.

She glanced up at her silent companion, striding carefully between the muddy pools of water and guiding her steps towards the coach waiting at the corner. And Jason, too, she thought, with his quiet, authoritative manner. The warm strength of his arm under hers, and his gentle, unquestioning control as he led her away from Whitehall, were immensely reassuring.

Then she caught sight of the ring on his little finger. It was the ring she had refused to accept from him. Topaz for fidelity. . . .